CASSIE MINT

Sweet Little Sinners: Books 1-4

BLACK CHERRY
PUBLISHING

Contents

III Honey Trap

IV Blade

1

Thief

Description

All I did was break into his penthouse… and try to steal a priceless jewel.

Now this billionaire's threatening to keep me.

I know, I know. It's cat burglar 101. Never break in while the owner is there!

Except I screwed up, and he caught my sticky fingers in the act. Now he won't let me leave until I fix the holes in his security.

I guess I should be grateful he's not calling the cops. And that he's feeding me, letting me sleep in his guest room, and giving me the world's best back rubs.

Is this weird? It feels kinda weird. But nice, too.

So, he won't let me leave until I help? Maybe I'll call his bluff.

Maybe I *want* to be his pet cat burglar.

Tabitha

⸙

I flop out of the suitcase onto hardwood floorboards, cheeks hot and breathing hard. It was *cramped* in there. Hot and dark and stifling. If I'd waited one more hour, my muscles would've locked.

There are more comfortable ways to break into an apartment, that's for sure. Picking locks or squeezing through windows. Wriggling through air conditioning shafts. But being carried in, zipped away in luggage or taped in a cardboard box—that's my favorite. They might as well roll out the welcome mat. So pleasing.

My joints pop as I stretch out my limbs, reveling in all this sudden space and fresh air. Spencer Arnoult's penthouse is dark, all silence and shadows, but even in the gloom I can tell this place is *nice*. Laying back on the hallway floorboards, I count four big paintings on the walls and a small sculpture of a cresting wave on a plinth.

Not what you'd expect from a tech bro, I'll give him that. I'd pictured purple neon floor lights and cheeto-dust fingerprints on everything. Framed posters of naked women and tentacle monsters. Instead, the apartment smells like orange blossom and night air, and the furnishings I can make out are downright tasteful.

So the guy's mature and artsy. I like that. There's nothing more depressing than a rich man's apartment filled with chrome and glass and nothing else—all white walls and sharp edges and zero personality. An airport lounge made chic.

I mean, I should know. I burgle enough of them.

Resting one palm on my stomach, I focus on slowing down my gasping breaths. Getting calm. Centered and ready. The most uncomfortable part of the night is over but my work has just begun, and the last thing I need is to be rushed and sloppy.

Somewhere in this penthouse is a priceless jewel. Spencer Arnoult bought it at auction last week, and in all his cocky glory, he didn't store it in a bank vault. He had it delivered *here*, to his apartment in the city. Practically dangled it under my nose.

And it's a beautiful jewel. A fist-sized sapphire the color of ocean mist. I'm going to find it, lick it, and keep it.

"C'mon, girl." I always time my little visits for when no one's home. It's safer, obviously, but it also means no one hears me talking to myself as I roll onto my side, stiff muscles aching, and push onto my hands and knees. This is part of the routine, too.

Cow pose.

Cat pose.

Downward facing dog.

If my burgling luck ever runs out, maybe I'll teach yoga in prison.

I'm still shaking out my stiff arms two minutes later, padding softly through Spencer Arnoult's kitchen. I never wear shoes to burgle. Can you imagine sharing that cramped suitcase with a pair of sneakers? Besides, shoes leave prints, and I don't leave clues behind. That's amateur hour. Black socks work just fine, along with black leggings, black gloves, a black long-sleeved top, and a black beanie to tuck away my long hair.

Hey, I like black. And it's kind of a uniform for burglars—not that there's anyone here to admire my outfit. I give a twirl anyway, even though it's just me and this marble-top kitchen island, this vintage wine rack, and this stainless steel refrigerator, my reflection spinning across the gleaming surface.

My steps pause.

My stomach growls.

Huh. I *am* pretty hungry. And burgling is hard work—it's non-stop adrenaline for days before and after.

Light spills across the kitchen tiles as I tug the refrigerator door open, peering in at Spencer Arnoult's shelves of food. God, I can never resist exploring when I break in somewhere, even when I'm on the clock. It's just so *delicious*, seeing behind the curtain like this. Sneaking behind enemy lines. It makes my insides go all tingly.

And you want to get to know a man? Take a look at his groceries. Here, one peek tells me that Spencer Arnoult has fine tastes, a healthy appetite, and probably cooks for himself. His shelves burst with fine cheeses and cured meats; pots of olives and fancy hummus. Ripe, colorful fruits and vegetables, rows of eggs, and glass bottles of milk.

Boring. But there's a carton of leftover takeout noodles tucked away at the back, and my flushed face melts into a smirk. *I* see you, Spencer Arnoult. Your veggies don't fool me.

I reach past the healthy stuff and snag the takeout container, pulling it down for a sniff.

Satay chicken. Fresh, too. *Hell* yeah.

One quick search for the microwave later, my surprise dinner hums as it heats up, spinning in the golden light. I lean against the kitchen island, sipping a tall glass of water, feeling so pleased with myself I could purr. Is this evil? I feel kind of evil. Not about the sapphire—no one *needs* one of those—but about stealing his leftovers.

I know if anyone ever dared rob *me*, that's what would piss me off most, right before I returned the favor. Because I treasure my leftovers. I lust over my meals for hours beforehand, imagining each perfect bite. Food takes up constant real estate in my brain, and I don't mean to brag, but it's a pretty big brain.

Stealing these leftovers... I'm not proud of it. Not exactly. But Spencer Arnoult is not here, and since he left town without those precious noodles, he clearly doesn't love them like I do.

So food first.

And maybe I'll dig through his bedroom drawers. A girl's gotta know.

Then I'll find the jewel. Easy peasy.

* * *

It's always surreal being inside a celebrity's private space. Not that I make a habit of burgling famous actors or whatever—not unless they have something pretty I really want—but wealthy people have their own orbit. It's impossible *not* to be aware of them, at least on some level.

And Spencer Arnoult has been in plenty of headlines over the last few years. He's been plastered over the twenty-four news cycle along with all those other Silicon Valley boy wonders, and though he left those roots behind when he came to this city in his mid-thirties, trading in his zip up hoodies for button-down shirts, his bank balance and billion dollar company came with him.

So I've seen his face plenty of times; I've heard his deep, stilted voice in interviews. I know *of* him. The man, the myth, the legend. That square jaw and the thick framed glasses. A stammering, pin-up Clark Kent.

And now I'm slurping his chicken satay noodles and sitting cross-legged on his couch, wriggling my sore ass against the cushions. His couch is forest green, covered in soft but sturdy fabric and draped with a fleecy cream throw.

It's kind of trashy, and I love it. He's got shockingly enjoyable taste. Sometimes I break into these penthouses and mansions, and there's so little personality I just want to scream at the off-white walls.

This place, though? It's homey. Fun yet soothing. Those other richies could learn a thing or two from Spencer Arnoult—and maybe I'll have to burgle him again. Come back and see what he's changed around the place.

I bite my lip as I prod the noodles with my fork. Peanut-scented steam curls over my cheeks, and I fish out a lump of chicken breast. How long did Frankie say he's away on business for? Three whole days?

Maybe I could stay the weekend, playing house with the ghost of a billionaire. There's plenty of food in the fridge.

Ha. Lil' old me, in an apartment like this. Could you ever imagine?

Spencer

There is someone in my home. *There is someone in my fucking home.* The thought rattles around my foggy brain, dragging me out of sleep; it pounds in my blood with every anxious squeeze of my heart. I know something is wrong the second I wake up with my face mashed into the pillows and the hairs raised on the back of my neck. My jaw is clenched and my muscles are tensed ready for a fight, and my back is damp with sweat.

I can't hear them yet. Can't hear anything but the shallow rasp of my own breath and the frantic *thud, thud, thud* of my heart.

But I know it. The same way you know there's someone nearby, even when they're not making a sound. *Especially* when they're not making a sound. It's the telltale, horrifying absence of noise.

Then my microwave gives a loud ping, and I choke back a panicked laugh. Some fucking burglar.

It's dark in here, the bed sheets tangled around my legs, and

10

I snatch my glasses off the nightstand, nearly jabbing my own eye in my rush to get them on. The weight of my cell phone is reassuring in my palm, my thumb blurring over the screen as I dial 911.

I'm not charging out there like Rambo. I wrestle code, not intruders, and only an idiot risks facing down a gun for the sake of their ego.

The operator is calm. Almost bored-sounding as she reels off a list of standard questions, including whether I have a roommate or a girlfriend or neighbors with thin walls. Basically, she's asking: *am I sure I'm not a dumbass?*

But this is the penthouse apartment. The only thing that ever knocks on my walls is the rough winds, storming high above the city. Still, I answer her questions in a hushed voice, straining for more sounds beyond my bedroom door.

There's nothing. For a horrible moment I think maybe I dreamed it, and I'll have to explain to a bunch of grumpy cops that I'm scared of things that go bump in the night. But then a sharp noise shatters the quiet: the unmistakable clatter of a fork dropped in my kitchen sink, and my muscles all tense rock hard again.

"The police will be with you in eight minutes, Mr Arnoult," the operator says, with no hint that she recognizes my name. Good. That's one less thing for my lawyer to worry about. I thank her and hang up, even as she invites me to stay on the line, and toss my phone to the mattress.

Eight minutes.

Eight long minutes.

A lot could happen in eight minutes.

* * *

I expect the burglar to ransack my apartment. To tear the valuable paintings off the walls and go through my electronics; maybe steal my laptop or copy my hard drive. I *definitely* expect them to go hunting for that damn sapphire I couldn't resist, but I still yelp in shock when they burst into my bedroom.

It's stupid, really. According to my schedule and everyone who knows my movements, I shouldn't be here tonight. The burglar clearly thinks they're alone since they ate my damn food, so why wouldn't they charge around like they own the place?

But there's nothing in my bedroom except *me,* my eyes wide and hair rumpled, hands raised in the universal sign for surrender. My burglar sucks in a shocked breath, slamming to a halt in the doorway, then tilts her head to the side.

Her head. Yeah. Because there's no mistaking that slender silhouette, framed by the light from my living room.

My burglar is a woman.

"Uh," I say, scanning her toned body for weapons, her lithe limbs dressed all in black. There's no gun, no glint of a blade, and apparently relief makes me even dumber than before, because I blurt, "Can I help you?"

She puffs out a laugh. She sounds winded, too, like this is too awful to believe. Well, fuck that. She's the one who broke in here, and my voice is harsh when I grind out, "The police are on their way."

Still no movement. No rush for the door.

Slowly, trying not to spook her, I switch on my bedside lamp—and it's my turn to lose all my air.

Because she's beautiful. Even in that ugly black beanie, she's so pretty she's hard to look at. With her creamy skin and pink

12

mouth and the tiny black mole on her upper lip, it's like staring directly into the sun. And when she sighs and tugs the hat off, caramel waves tumbling around her shoulders, I forget how to swallow.

My shoulder blades press against the headboard. I tug the bed covers over my lap.

"I was thinking about teaching yoga in prison earlier," my burglar tells me, casually wandering into my bedroom like we really are roommates. "I jinxed it. Such a rookie error." She wanders to the window, pulling back the dark drapes to stare at the streets below, and she doesn't seem stressed. Just lost in her own thoughts.

"I'm sorry," I rasp, though fuck knows why I'm commiserating with her. "I do that sometimes with important meetings. I picture myself screwing it all up, and then I play it out exactly the same way. Like I wrote myself a script."

She smiles at me, clearly charmed, and lets the curtain drop. "Not many powerful men would admit that, Spencer Arnoult."

I shrug one shoulder, not sure what to say. I don't like many powerful men, even though theoretically they're my peers. They're too concerned with hurting people to prove they can—like little boys frying ants under a magnifying glass. I've been that ant. I *won't* be that man. "How do you—"

I cut myself off with an irritated grunt. *How do you know my name?* That's what I was about to ask, like she's a girl I bumped into at a party or a bar like a normal person. But of course she knows my fucking name. She's here to burgle me. She probably knows every single thing about me—everything worth stealing, anyway.

"Aren't you going to run?" I ask her instead, and my beautiful thief shakes her head, her golden hair shifting against those shoulders.

Those *shoulders*. Those arms, those legs, Jesus Christ. I didn't know I liked sculpted muscles on women until I met my burglar, and now I'm mentally subscribing to Sports Illustrated even as I can't tear my eyes away from her. She looks like she wandered off the Olympics gymnastics team.

"There's no point. I didn't plan for a quick escape, you know? I thought I'd have hours to get around your security system and work my way down to the lobby. The fact is, Spencer," she flops onto the edge of my bed, kicking out her legs and crossing her ankles, "I've screwed up. I'll go down with dignity."

I stare at her feet. "You're not wearing any shoes."

She wiggles her toes in those black socks. "Nope. Wouldn't have been comfy in the suitcase."

"In the—" I break off, pinching the bridge of my nose. I got a load of old cases delivered from storage this morning. But that was hours ago, and the delivery men were not exactly gentle. She was in there that whole time? Is she dehydrated?

I prod at my phone, checking the time on the screen. Four minutes until the cops arrive. "You really should run," I tell her. "I'll help you past the security system, but you're on your own from there."

I don't examine why I so desperately want to help her. Why I *need* to get her out of here before a bunch of pushy, forceful police barge in here and grab her, push her around, shout at her and put her slender wrists in handcuffs...

"Spencer." Her soft voice cuts through my rising stress, and a small, gloved hand slips into mine. "Don't worry, okay? I got caught, fair and square, and I knew the risks. You shouldn't feel guilty."

This is the weirdest conversation of my life.

But it only gets stranger as she lets out a huff, collapsing back on the bed and resting her head on my thigh. I stare at her for what feels like an eternity, then smooth a cautious palm over her hair. It feels like warm silk.

My burglar hums. She squirms closer, her hand still in mine.

When was the last time I touched someone like this? When was the last time *I* was touched like this, with affection and intimacy and no underlying motives? I don't remember.

I really don't remember, and now that I've had this tiny taste, my body is screaming for more. My chest aches and my skin flushes and I want ten more minutes with her holding my hand. Ten more minutes, and I'd trade anything. She can take the stupid sapphire. *Anything*.

"Please run," I grit out. "Please. I wish I never called them. I thought—I thought you were some asshole with a gun."

She nods, squeezing my fingers. "You did the right thing. That would have been dangerous."

God. I swallow hard, and my throat is tight. Outside, in the street far below, faint sirens approach the building.

"Please…"

"Tabitha," she supplies. Her pink lips curve into a smile as she watches me, staring like she's as fascinated by this connection as I am.

I grip her hand tighter, willing her to listen to me, damn it. "Please, Tabitha. I'm begging you. Go."

"Nope." She pops the 'p', and I huff and bend forward, my forehead touching hers.

"They might be rough with you." I can barely say the words.

But: "I'll handle it," she murmurs, and *no*. I can't be part of this. I won't allow it, won't let her get hurt on my behalf. I don't care what she's done, don't care what laws she's broken.

15

When a fist pounds on my apartment door, I'm already resolved.

"Wait here," I tell her, brushing a kiss on her forehead. My face is hot as I straighten, nudging her up so I can climb out of bed. "I mean it. Don't go anywhere."

Her soft laugh follows me out of the room. "Jeez, Spencer. Make up your mind."

Tabitha

❧

Do I want to go to prison? Nope. No, thank you. I don't look good in jumpsuits, and I hate cafeteria food. If I can avoid it at all, I'll opt out.

But do I want Spencer Arnoult to watch me get hurt trying to make some mad escape, then blame himself for the rest of his painfully sweet life?

…No. I want that even less.

I don't know what's come over me. I'm not the sentimental type, and I'm not protective. I don't throw myself under the bus for strangers. But this guy? This shy, blushing man with his broad shoulders and that muscle flexing in his jaw? Turns out he's got some weird power over me.

Maybe it's guilt for eating his chicken satay noodles, the one comfort food in his kitchen—or maybe it's the way my head feels pillowed against his strong thigh. Whatever it is, when the cops bang on his door, I'm already resolved. I'll make this easier for him, however I can. I owe him that.

"Wait here," he says, brushing a kiss against my forehead

that reverberates down to my freaking soul. "I mean it. Don't go anywhere."

Sure. It's not like my limbs work after the shock of that kiss, anyway. I let him up, then blink at his toned ass in his dark striped pajama pants as he walks away.

I'm glad I ate those noodles, actually. Spencer can always order more, and that might be my last free meal before prison. My mouth twists as I peer around his bedroom, looking for a safe or a lock box.

I wonder where he keeps that sapphire.

Not that I could get it now, but call it professional curiosity. What other treasures does he keep in this penthouse? My limbs are wobbly as I flop onto my side, tugging his nightstand drawer open. Voices echo down the hall.

A box of tissues and a pot of lube. An old phone charger, a battered sci fi paperback, and an unopened box of condoms.

Oh, Spencer. I smile, chest raw, and nudge the drawer closed. *You're breaking my heart.*

For his sake, I kind of wish I'd found something salacious in there. Instead, he seems even lonelier to me than before.

I meant what I said. When the cops come in here, I won't put up a fight. I'll present my wrists like a good little burglar, and retain the final scraps of my dignity. But they're taking their sweet time, talking in low, clipped voices in the hall, and waiting for my freedom to end is driving me crazy.

I lurch to my feet, heart racing. I'll go easy. I will.

But I won't sit here and mope for the final minutes before my arrest.

* * *

Spencer's other nightstand is empty except for a single used battery and a mothball. I stride past his closet and go into his en suite bathroom next, tugging open the mirrored cabinet above the sink.

Shaving cream and a razor. Contact lenses and solution. Aspirin and toothpaste and mouthwash and soap and every other boring thing you'd expect to find. Ugh.

I shut the cabinet with a growl. This guy is so freaking normal. Doesn't he know that billionaires are supposed to be unhinged? So what am I looking for here? What would make me feel better?

Something shiny, maybe. Or a secret. Some private piece of knowledge about Spencer Arnoult to tuck away inside myself and dwell on during my years behind bars. I prowl to the laundry hamper, flipping the lid open and frowning at the empty space.

No pants pockets to dig through. Probably for the best.

"Tabitha." Spencer's deep voice bounces off the bathroom tiles. "What are you… are you looking through my laundry?"

"No." I snap the lid closed, waving a hand at the empty hamper. "I tried but there's nothing in there."

Spencer Arnoult splutters as I wheel around and stalk to the shower.

They must be coming, right? If Spencer's here, the cops must be right behind him, and these are my final seconds to explore, to learn about him, to be *free*. My time's slipping away, trickling like water through my fingers.

I yank the glass door open, stick my head inside the large cubicle and suck in a deep breath. His shampoo smells like green apple. God, why'd he have to be so cute?

"Tabitha. The sapphire's next to the soap."

19

I jerk my head up to look, and behind me, Spencer chuckles. The jewel's not in his shower, obviously. I'm not thinking straight. Partly because of my looming imprisonment, and partly because he's moved closer, his bare feet silent on the bathroom tiles.

Spencer Arnoult would make a decent cat burglar.

"Why aren't they coming in?" I whisper over the rush of blood in my ears. I talked a big game, acted all calm and confident earlier, but the longer this drags out, the harder my heart pounds. Forget these final seconds and forget finding one last secret. I just want to get this over with.

"I told them I made a mistake. That there's no intruder." Spencer pauses. "They are not my biggest fans right now."

I frown at the shower tiles. "Why would you do that?" I feel like my hacker friend Frankie when strangers try to make small talk: *Does not compute.*

But Spencer sighs and rests a palm on my shoulder—and god, his *heat*. This man is a walking furnace. I didn't realize before in his bedroom, but in this cool, tiled room? A groan crowds up my throat and I choke it back.

Must not melt back against the billionaire.

Must not wrap his arms around my waist.

"I figured we could make a deal."

He sounds so reasonable. I bet this is how he makes all those brutal business deals for his tech company. He pulls his sweet, reasonable, puppy dog act and then *bam.* Everyone's eating out of his palm and they don't even know it.

"You got in here with no trouble, so there are obviously holes in my security. I'll let the attempted burglary go, and in return, you can help me secure my home."

My heart sinks. I scowl at the shower head, eyes dry.

Well, what the hell did I think Spencer Arnoult wanted from me? He's right. I came here to rob him, and that's all.

"That's blackmail."

"Hardly." The hand on my shoulder squeezes gently, and my eyelids drift closed. Damn, that feels good on my stiff muscles. "You're the one who broke in here, and I'm offering you a way out. But if you prefer to think of it like that... well, you're not exactly a champion of legality, Tabitha."

See what I mean? Puppy dog, then *bam.*

My mouth twitches. I like this guy. "What about the sapphire?"

Spencer hums. "What about it?"

My cheeks lift as I grin wider. He's still touching my shoulder. "If I find it, can I keep it?"

There's a long pause, and the soft shift of his weight. Spencer comes up right behind me, his hard chest at my back, and when he hovers his lips by my ear, his warm breath tickles my neck.

"Is that how it works, Tabitha? Finders keepers?"

Strong arms snake around my waist, and I hold on to them for balance. "It is in my world."

Spencer grunts. His arms tighten. "Well, I found *you.*"

Oh, god. I'm not... I'm not shiny or precious. I'm not someone people want to collect, not really. Not once they get to know me. Because I'm a charming kleptomaniac who ate his treasured satay noodles, and he doesn't even know about that betrayal yet.

He will, though. He won't hug me again after that.

So Spencer Arnoult doesn't want to keep me. He's messing with me, trying to make me agree to his deal. Except, even if that's true... why am I being so difficult about this? I owe him big time. This could have turned out so much worse, and if

I'm honest with myself, I don't *want* to leave. Not yet.

So, spending a few days with the tech billionaire?

Poking around in his apartment, digging up secrets and shiny treasures?

Ordering those chicken satay noodles again?

Sign me up. I'm so in.

"I need to get a message to someone," I tell his hand, playing with Spencer's squared, manly thumb. Rubbing circles on the knuckle and watching him stroke me back. Every tiny point of contact scorches my skin. "I should tell them I'm safe but delayed."

There's an approving rumble. "Well, we're not short on tech."

He takes my hand, our fingers tangling together, and I follow him out of the bathroom, dazed and lightheaded.

In and out. Grab the sapphire and go.

Yeah, right. This did not go according to plan.

Spencer

I am, theoretically, a very smart man. I have the IQ and the advanced degrees in computing to prove it; the successful companies and the eye-watering bank balance. But riddle me this: is it smart to put your would-be burglar in a guest room for the night and leave her there unattended?

No. *No.* It is very obviously not smart. But I do it anyway, because a big, dumb part of me desperately wants to trust Tabitha.

The worst part is, I don't trust her not to steal from me. Not at all. I saw the desperate gleam in her eye as she probed around my bathroom—on some level, it must be compulsive. But I don't *care* about that stuff. When I say I want to trust her, I mean I want to trust her not to leave.

Or at least, to tell me she's going. To say goodbye. To leave her number and text me when she gets home safely.

See what I mean? I'm a grade A dumbass.

I lie in bed until dawn, staring at the shadowed ceiling and wondering what she's doing in the other room. Is she asleep? Is she lying awake, wondering about me too? Or is she creeping around my penthouse, stuffing valuables in one of those black sacks burglars carry in cartoons, with tiny dollar signs floating in her sea-mist eyes?

Maybe if I bought more jewels and hid them around my apartment, she'd visit me again.

Fuck. I need therapy.

It's a relief when the pale light of dawn creeps around the edges of my curtains. I jump out of bed like a loaded spring, stride into my en suite and crank the shower on. With one hand braced against the tiles and the other wrapped around my cock, I screw my eyes shut and try to conjure her husky voice saying my name; the warm silk of her hair; those big blue eyes blinking up at me, her head pillowed on my thigh.

Those curves. Those muscles. Those thick, gymnast thighs. Her smaller hand wrapped in mine, squeezing my fingers as she smiled.

I choke back a groan, streaking the shower tiles with white.

It's been so long since anyone touched me casually; since I was treated as an organic being and not just an email address. Tabitha's hand in mine was a lifeline I didn't realize I needed.

* * *

"Well. This is an obvious weak point." Tabitha stands in my hallway, one hand on her hip, the other holding a slice of buttered toast. She munches as we stare down at the empty suitcase she left abandoned on my floorboards last night.

Damn, this girl can eat. I made her pancakes with scrambled eggs and crispy bacon for breakfast, and she ate every bite then still made toast before we headed out on our little security tour. Mental note: cook large portions for Tabitha. I guess burgling is a calorie burner.

"I can't believe you fit in there." Tabitha arches an eyebrow, chewing slowly, and heat crawls up my throat. "I don't—I didn't mean—it's a suitcase, Tabitha! Come on, how the fuck did you even fit?"

She swallows her mouthful and hands me her half-eaten toast, brushing the crumbs off the faded Pac-Man t-shirt she 'borrowed' this morning while I was in the shower. "Don't eat that."

I roll my eyes as she steps into the suitcase. She's very territorial for a thief. "God forbid."

Watching Tabitha contort like a pretzel, bending those lithe limbs and folding herself into the small space, confirms to me that yes, under it all, I'm just a man. A horny, basic, shameless man, because I want her pretzeled like this in the center of my bed, her ankles hooked behind her ears, and I want to tear her leggings open and lick her until she cries.

Tabitha grins at me from her tangle. "You're blushing, Spencer."

I take a bite of her toast. Her eyes narrow. "If that was the extra buttery bit—"

"It was."

Her angry huffing is undercut by the ungraceful way she flops onto the floorboards.

"I can't believe that didn't wake me last night," I muse. "You're so loud getting out."

"I'm not trying to be quiet just now."

"You weren't trying last night either. You used my microwave." The memory of the empty takeout carton flashes across my mind, and I take another large bite of her toast. I'm not hungry, but I am bitter. I wanted those noodles.

"Hey!" Tabitha grabs my legs for balance, lurching to her feet. She snatches the final crust, then stuffs it in her face like a hamster.

There's a crumb in the corner of her mouth. Alarm bells ring in my skull.

Do not even think about it, Arnoult. Do not lick that crumb.

Because holding her hand is one thing; stealing touches here and there seems okay. But kissing her while I'm basically holding her captive? No, I don't think so. I don't want to be some creepy comic book villain. This is weird enough already.

"So how did you know about the suitcases?" I ask her instead as she smooths her clothes and tosses back her caramel hair. Her eyes are narrowed, and something about them feels familiar. It nags at the back of my brain.

The sapphire. It hits me like a slap: the sapphire is the exact shade of Tabitha's eyes.

"Your emails," she says, bringing me slamming back to earth. She knew about the suitcases because of my emails.

Of course. Nothing online is truly secure—I know that better than anyone.

"So you hacked me." I'm oddly disappointed. It's such an anticlimax.

"No, a friend hacked you ages ago. She keeps tabs on things in the city, you know, likes to see what the movers and shakers are doing. Then when I saw you bought that sapphire, I asked her to find me a way in. She told me about the cases being moved from storage, and she knows I like being carried inside the places I burgle, so we arranged for my case to be added in transit."

It's clean. Simple. Why did I want lasers and blueprints and elevator shafts? I don't even *have* lasers.

"You're disappointed," Tabitha says, and shit, she sees way too much. Her arms fold over her chest. "You wanted me to be a burglar like in the movies. Cooler and sexier."

"Not possible," I grit out, because she's right, that's so dumb, and a cooler, sexier Tabitha would surely break the laws of physics. "Tell me: why do you like being carried inside?"

Those pink lips curl into a smirk. "It's funny."

Fuck. It *is* funny. And she's so irreverent, so sly, that I can't get enough of her. I just want to ply her with take out food for weeks on end and listen to every story she has. How long can I drag this deal out? How long can I keep her?

As if she can hear my thoughts, Tabitha wanders to the front door. According to her plan, she would have worked her way past my security system last night, albeit with several hours to figure it out.

"Go on." I crowd closer, the green apple scent of my shampoo clinging to her damp hair. My hands find their way to her hips, and I rub her waist with my thumbs. "Show me how you'd get past it."

Tabitha frowns at the white box by my door. It's deceptively simple-looking, but she must know that it's top of the range. It's coded to my fingerprint, or a ten-digit pin only I know, and if she can't get past it, maybe I really *could* keep her. It's an ugly thought, but I think it anyway.

She prods at the alarm. "This is our deal, right? I help you with your security, then you let me out."

Shit. "I… yeah, I guess so. That's what we said." Honestly, I'd have said anything if it meant keeping Tabitha here for a few more hours. I'd have signed over the deed to my apartment.

There's a long silence. It stretches on and on, until my skin feels too hot under my white t-shirt, and I push my glasses up the bridge of my nose in a nervous tic. And still she stares at the alarm, head cocked but her expression far away.

Then: "Nope." Tabitha spins on her heel, marching back down the hall. She sidesteps the suitcase easily, her caramel hair dancing against her back. "Not today. I don't feel like helping you right now, Spencer Arnoult."

I make a strangled noise, following after her. What does that even mean? Is our deal off? "Why not?" I call, exasperated.

She throws a smirk over her shoulder. "It'll make things harder for me next time."

Next time?

Hope and frustration war inside me as I trail her into the living room.

This woman will drive me insane.

Tabitha

I can't leave until I help him? Well, maybe I don't *want* to leave, so I'll call his bluff. How about that, Spencer Arnoult? Because last night was the first time in weeks that I slept soundly, curled up in a strange guest bedroom and knowing he was near. Plus there's all that food in the fridge. Those vintage wines. And that sapphire is in this penthouse somewhere…

But it's Spencer, really. I can't lie to myself. I want to stay closer to him, at least for a little while longer.

I figure he'll be angry at my refusal to help. That he'll storm out and go to work, or maybe even call the cops again.

What I *don't* expect is for him to cancel all his work for the day, put on a movie, then bundle me onto the sofa. He even pulls my legs into his lap and tucks the fleecy throw around my bare feet, then hands me the remote and tells me to change it to anything I want.

I leave it on the cheesy monster movie he put on. I'm not really watching anyway; I'm too busy soaking up Spencer's warmth and inching closer to him under the blanket.

He's got that sexy nerd thing *down*. Under his white cotton t-shirt, his muscles are hard and defined, and I bite my lip every time that he reaches for something and his shape is briefly clearer under the fabric. And that thick, dark hair? Those black-framed glasses? God, I just want to steam those lenses right over. I want to pull his hair and make him growl.

My favorite thing about Spencer Arnoult, though, is that he can't keep his freaking hands off me. It's like a nervous tic, or something. I'm his girl-sized safety blanket. Every second, he's either rubbing his thumb on my ankle or massaging my feet; he's stroking a palm up and down my shin or wrapping an arm around my shoulders.

Halfway through the movie, I pull my legs out of his lap. Spencer actually looks disappointed—until I spin around and rest my back against his chest instead.

Then those big, warm hands land on my shoulders, and I get the best back rub of my freaking life.

"Oh, shit. Spencer. Holy shit." My head lolls like I'm drunk. He laughs behind me, darkly delighted, and tingles race through my body.

"I guess hours in a suitcase aren't good for the muscles."

"Nope." I grip his thigh and squeeze, panting as he keeps kneading my stiff shoulders. "Oh my god."

"Tabitha." My billionaire sounds strained. I jolt and remove my fingernails from his hard thigh. "No, I—put those back." I squeeze him even tighter this time, and his low hiss does things to me. I like bossy Spencer. It suits him. "Tabitha, is this… tell me this is okay."

"It's okay," I groan, because how is that not blindingly obvious? I've plastered myself all over him; I'm practically grinding in his lap. I'm surrounded by Spencer's heat and scent and low, rumbly growls, and yep, I'm in heaven. "It's more than okay. It's... I..."

I can't think. Can't string a sentence together. This is more than I've been touched in the last year, and it's frying my circuits. Fritzing my brain.

"Yeah," Spencer chokes out. "It is." His thumbs dig deeper into my shoulders, and I nearly howl. I scramble sideways, sitting fully in his lap, and the movie is long, long forgotten.

"Turn around," Spencer orders, then goes *oof* when I accidentally knee him in the gut. We don't stop, though. He keeps his hands on me, roaming and squeezing and *owning* me until I'm straddling him nose-to-nose, my ass perched on his thighs. The throw is somewhere on the floor.

I loop my arms around his neck. His cheekbones are tinged pink.

"This is not part of the deal," Spencer grates out. "You don't have to do this."

I shut him up, slamming my mouth on his. I don't want to hear that. Of course this isn't some transaction. This is...

I whimper, kissing him harder. It's everything.

"Tabby," Spencer groans, pulling away to suck kisses down my throat. "Tabby the cat burglar. Shit. I just got that."

"Stop talking."

"You are very cat-like."

His hair is soft as I pull it, guiding his face back to mine. "*Spencer.*"

I want him to devour me whole. I want him surrounding me, overwhelming my senses, and I want his tongue sliding against mine. I want the hard line of his cock beneath my ass, and the way his hips twitch up like he can't help it, and I want

31

the low, breathless sounds he makes.

Spencer wraps my hair around his fist.

Oh, *jackpot.*

"Do what you want," I babble, half drunk on him. "Do whatever you want to me."

He pauses, chest heaving. "Slow down."

No! Shit. I don't want to slow down. I've never been good at putting the brakes on. I like risk and adrenaline and going a hundred miles per hour. Riding shotgun in the car chase of life. And fine, maybe this is all new to me, but I *want* it. I'm not good at impulse control.

"Spencer," I whine, rocking myself in his lap. "You feel so good. Don't you want to?"

His laugh is broken as he plucks my arms from around his neck. He holds my wrists in front of me, gentle but firm, echoing the handcuffs I nearly wore. "Trust me. Like you wouldn't believe."

"Then why—"

"We can," he promises, and the sharp ache in my chest eases a little. "And we will, if you want to. But not yet."

Not yet. Psh. "Why wait if we both want it?" I sound pouty and irritated, but I can't help it. This sexy nerd is a tease. He dangled his Clark Kent dimples and his hidden abs and his delicious manly scent, and now he's snatching them all away again.

"It's called delayed gratification, Tabitha." He raises an eyebrow. "Like how stuffing yourself in a suitcase for twelve hours is worth it for that first stretch when you're free."

I blink at his serious green eyes. He does paint a vivid picture. Because if this is how good it feels after a few minutes, imagine if we waited. Imagine if he teased me more.

"You're an evil genius," I whisper.

Spencer smirks, his thumbs tracing circles on my wrists. "Don't believe all the headlines."

So… waiting. Sure. I can wait for something good.

How hard can it be?

* * *

I need to find that sapphire. I need *something*, damn it, because I'm going out of my freaking mind. All day, Spencer's been stroking my arms and kissing my neck. Licking my pulse points. Pressing me against the wall and smelling my hair. He's been winding me up like a clockwork toy, then whenever I'm about to snap, whenever I'm pushing back against him, slick and aching and ready to beg…

He walks away.

"I hate you," I tell him as he does it again, leaving me draped over the kitchen island.

"No, you don't," he says, prising his laptop open on the counter, then typing quickly before carrying it over and setting it beside me. On the screen is the menu for a take out place. The land of chicken satay noodles. "Would you like your own food? Or would you prefer to steal mine?"

He's probably joking, but I consider the question. I like picking my own meals, yes, but there is truly nothing more delicious than stolen food. A hot, salty fry swiped from someone else's plate? Paradise.

"Maybe I could choose half your food," I say slowly, "and you could order double."

He laughs, loud and bright. Like I'm delightful rather than crazed. "Sure, yeah. I guess I'm extra hungry tonight."

I roll my eyes and scroll through the menu, adding the dishes I want to steal from him to the cart. He wants the full Tabitha experience? This is it. This is all me. And that's a scary thought, one that steals my breath and makes my ears ring, but if Spencer notices, he doesn't comment. He spins the laptop back to face him and adds more food, then snaps the lid shut.

"Order confirmed. Now don't go thinking I'll make it easy on you." His mouth quirks, and he looks kind of evil as he drums his fingers on the counter. "I'm gonna fight you for that food."

I poke my tongue out, and when he turns away, I collapse forward on the island.

Oh, god.

This is it. I'm in love.

Spencer

'*ve left my burglar needy for a long, long time today. I've been teasing her non-stop for hours, working her into a trembling, gasping mess and then leaving her unfulfilled, and I think if I do it one more time, Tabitha might actually kill me.

"Please," she groans just after midnight, stretched out on my bed with her arms tossed over her head. I'm straddling her waist, one palm pressed against her bare stomach, her flushed skin damp with sweat. "Oh my god. Have mercy."

The Pac-Man t-shirt is in a crumpled heap on the floor next to mine. Our lips are bruised and swollen from rough kisses, and the late night stars wink through my windows. I'm acting calm and unruffled, but honestly, I don't know how much longer I can take this either. I'm so hard, the zipper of my jeans is gonna leave tiny bite marks on my cock.

"You've been so patient," I rasp, and Tabitha chokes out a laugh. Yeah, that's a lie. My beautiful, impulsive thief hasn't been patient at all. She's thrown hourly tantrums, whining for my touch, and fuck, I love that she wants this so badly. That she's not embarrassed to tell me so.

I want her, too. More than my next breath. More than anything.

Enough teasing. I can't drag this out any longer.

Slowly, softly, I draw a line down the center of her body, from the hollow of her throat over her sports bra and rib cage, all the way down to the waistband of her leggings. As I go, she undulates under my path. Ripples up to press my finger against her harder.

I smirk. "Time for your reward."

She's hot and slick already. Dewy with sweat.

Her eyes bore into me, wide and pleading. "Yes. Give it to me."

I know what Tabitha means, but that's not what she's getting. Not tonight. She wants my cock slamming inside her, my hips pumping while her toes curl, and yeah, *soon*, we'll do that soon. But if I give her everything she wants right now, what reason does she have left to stay?

I might as well hand her the sapphire, pat her on the head, and unlock the door. And I can't face that reality. Can't handle the thought of her gone.

So I move down her body. Hook my fingers over her waistband, then peel her leggings down her thighs.

I blink at the sight before me. She's pink and slick and puffy. Swollen with need. "No underwear?"

Tabitha hums and spreads her legs wider, pleased at my attention. She rocks her hips from side to side. "I didn't exactly bring an overnight bag."

"Lie still." I grab her hips, because that's way too distracting. She giggles. "I'm going to use my mouth on you. Okay?"

36

I can hear the pout in her voice, even though I'm staring at her pussy. "Just your mouth? *Spencer.*"

My heart's beating faster against my ribs. "My fingers too."

"Ugh."

I grin at her strip of caramel curls, running my fingers through the golden hair. She's such a brat. "If you don't tell me that's okay, you won't get any of it."

I glance up in time to catch her eyes, and if looks could kill, I'd be a lump of ash on the bed sheets. "*Fine.* Okay."

She can act like a martyr, but when I draw my tongue along her seam, Tabitha melts against the bed in pure bliss. I lick her deep, sloppy and sinful, all the way from her ass to her clit, and her thighs are shiny with her arousal. Her musk hangs in the air.

"Gonna eat you up," I murmur, my breath wafting against her folds. "Have to. You ate half my dinner."

Tabitha laughs weakly, swatting at my shoulder. And I *love* that laugh, but I love her gasps and moans too. The little broken whimpers she makes. The way she chokes out my name, like forming words is too difficult and she can only manage that one. The creak of the headboard as she holds on for dear life. All her sounds.

My jaw clicks, but I don't care. And I can't really breathe, but who needs oxygen?

I press her thighs wider, my fingertips digging cruel points in her flesh.

"Oh!" she gasps when my teeth graze her clit. "Do that—do that again."

I spank her ass, then do as she says, and her hips are rocking beneath me, her whole body chasing my tongue.

"You taste fucking amazing," I mumble, buried eyebrow-

37

deep. She's salty and sweet, just like the rest of her.

"What?" Tabby says.

I shrug and keep licking. Never mind.

As I pin her down, working her into a shuddery, gasping mess, Tabitha's thick thighs creep up around my shoulders. She traps me tighter and tighter, until she's muffling every sound, and all I can hear is my heartbeat thudding in my ears and the distant creak of the bed.

She could snap my neck and I'd die happy down here. What a way to go.

Like I said. I need therapy.

I risk a glance up her body, over her valleys and hills, her chest heaving, and find her squeezing her own tits. Plucking her nipples through the fabric of her sports bra. Fuck, that's hot.

I slide one finger into her channel. Not far—to the second knuckle. Just enough to drive her mad.

Tabitha howls and yanks on my hair. "Stop! Teasing!"

Two fingers thrust all the way together, pumping in and out, rubbing her walls. And I'm lapping her steadily, tormenting her clit with the flat of my tongue, and my groan vibrates against her sensitive flesh. Fuck, this was worth waiting for.

I add a third finger, squeezing her ass cheek hard with the other hand. I graze her clit once more with my teeth, then suck it into my mouth.

"Oh. Oh!"

She arches off the bed, shaking, her eyes screwed shut and her teeth clenched. Fluid drips down my chin, and I still don't let up. I lick her like I'm punishing her for something. Like I'm getting revenge for how she makes me feel.

Because I'm raw, and desperate, and so fucking hungry

for every touch. Like an addict hooked on the world's most intoxicating drug.

Mine, I tell her with every lick. *Mine, mine, mine.*

All at once, Tabitha collapses. Just like that, it's over. She falls back like a puppet with cut strings, and then she's smacking me off, pushing me away with muttered curses.

"Enough. Enough, already. God. My ears are ringing."

Good. I crawl up her body, then collapse by her side. My chin and cheeks are slick, but I make no move to wipe them clean. I like it too much. The sticky sensation of her on my skin.

My cock presses so hard against my fly, my head pounds. I flick my button open. "Do you mind if I…?"

"Yes, I mind." She bats my hand away, then tugs my zipper down. Draws my cock out herself. Her grip is inexpert, but it won't take much. I was half a breath away from blowing in my pants the whole time I was licking her.

"Tabby," I grit out. "Grip me harder. Yeah."

She smiles, so sly, and adds a cruel little twist with each pump. "You like it mean, Spencer."

I curl over, like I'm winded. Fuck, that's good. "Shit. You know I do."

Two more twists, and I'm spilling over her hand. Streaking her fingers with white. Tabitha works me through it all, and when I'm done, she sucks her fingers into her mouth one by one.

Look at us both. Boneless and breathless and sticky. Two people stripped back to our most primal instincts.

"We should shower," I rasp after what feels like ten years. "The good news is there's laundry now for you to paw through. No sapphire, though."

She flicks my nipple hard enough to sting.

My body is languid, but my heart is hollow as I trail her to the bathroom. There's only one thing left that she wants from me. Two if I count the jewel—and I'd be a fool not to.

And after that? My heart sinks as I crank the water on. What could I possibly offer this girl?

Tabitha

Here are the things I've stolen from Spencer Arnoult since breaking into his penthouse: his chicken satay noodles. A Pac-Man t-shirt. A pair of platinum cuff links. My dinner. Two sets of fancy wireless headphones. Engraved chopsticks. A fountain pen. A first edition Asimov hardback. Socks. A small ornate vase.

And here's what he's stolen from me: my freaking heart.

So. He wins.

After we collapse back into bed, Spencer falls asleep right away. Seriously, it's like someone flipped a light switch and he's gone, lips parted and soft breaths shifting his broad chest. One arm curls against his waist, the other reaches blindly across the mattress for me. He looks younger without his glasses, though the lines at the corners of his eyes give him away.

But I guess that's what happens when you're not a walking bundle of guilt and shame. You can lie back, close your eyes and drift off to sleep, sweet and easy.

Yeah, that never happens for me. I'm a toss-and-turn, grind my teeth, huff at the ceiling and give up before dawn kinda girl. Three guesses why.

The penthouse is silent when I crawl back out of bed, tossing away the covers and stalking to the bathroom. Moonlight shines through the frosted window and bounces off the mirrored cabinet, and I tug the door open and stare at the contents, even though I already know what I'll find.

Boring things. Innocent things.

I shut the cabinet with a growl.

The laundry hamper stares at me, but I don't go in there again. I cross to the bathroom shelves instead, stacked with fluffy green towels and an unlit scented candle, but when I slide the towels apart, there's no sign of a lock box.

I try the living room next, opening every thick book on the bookcase, checking for hidden compartments. I feel around all the lampshades, kneel down and check beneath the sofa, and open every slot on the gaming console.

The sapphire won't be hidden like this. It's a precious jewel, not a preteen's diary. But I can't resist looking anyway, turning Spencer's penthouse inside out, and with each passing minute I feel worse.

What the hell is wrong with me? Why am I like this?

Why can't I go back in there and sleep beside him?

I don't know what messed up part of my brain makes me need to do this, makes me poke and pry and steal in order to find a semblance of calm, but whatever the reason, Spencer Arnoult deserves better.

He's asleep because he trusts me. I'm out here because he shouldn't.

Ugh. Bad Tabitha.

I find the sapphire in his study, because of course I do. There's a safe concealed under his desk, because Spencer is a normal person who stores valuables in appropriate places.

The safe takes me twenty three minutes to crack. I'm just so fuzzy, I can't think straight. And when I get it open, when I pull that stormy pale blue jewel out into the lamplight, I feel… nothing.

I'm hollow. Sad.

I flop down into Spencer's desk chair and spin the sapphire in my fingertips. It's so pretty, so sparkly; it's everything I wanted when I decided to target this man. And now that I've got it, I only wish that I never found it.

I place the sapphire gently on the center of Spencer's desk, my throat tight and aching, then rummage in his drawers for a notepad and pen. Dry-eyed, I stare blankly at the wall for five minutes, then scrawl the only thing I can think to say.

I leave the rest of my stolen goods in a pile on the guest bed. All except for the Pac-Man t-shirt. It's too faded, too comfy, and it smells faintly of Spencer, and even in my newfound control, I can't resist that.

I shrug the t-shirt on, wander back to the bathroom with a roll of sticky tape, and lift one of Spencer's fingerprints from the mirror. High security? Please.

This t-shirt looks too small for him anyway. He's got such deliciously broad shoulders.

So… sue me.

* * *

"You look like hell."

Five days later, Frankie stands at my door, her arms piled

43

high with bags of candy and glossy magazines. Her brown hair is pulled into a topknot, her bangs ruffled from the wind, and she's in her daily uniform of baggy sweatpants and a loose tank, a soft cardigan draped around her slender shoulders.

She raises her armload, candy bags rustling. "I looked it up. This is what friends are supposed to do in a personal crisis."

My apartment door creaks as I pull it wide, waving her in, and Frankie peers around my small living room and faded red sofa. It's all soft rugs and bare brick. Understated charm.

I may steal priceless treasures, but I keep my lifestyle modest. It deflects unwanted attention, but Frankie doesn't get that. She *loves* living in a flashy city apartment, piling onto the elevator with a bunch of wealthy CEOs and fancy lawyers, shocking them with her sweatpants and bright purple high-tops. But Frankie doesn't have a buttload of stolen goods in her apartment—only a tricked out computer.

"Apparently, we're supposed to watch cheesy movies and do our nails."

I frown down at my chewed-on stubs. "Do we have to?"

"Yes."

Once Frankie internalizes a social rule, that's it. We're done for. That's how I find myself cross-legged on the sofa thirty minutes later, a high school comedy blaring on the TV and a pot of nail polish wedged beside my calf. I grimace as I dab a glob of emerald polish onto my thumb nail, the messy stroke spilling onto my skin. "Shit."

"You'd think as a thief you'd have steadier hands."

I grunt, moving onto my index finger.

"We can talk about him, you know," Frankie offers. "I looked up the right things to say."

Even so, the aching hollow in my chest says we can't.

Whenever I think about Spencer, even for a minute, every breath hurts. My bones throb; my stomach churns. I miss him so badly, it doesn't seem like it should be possible. Better to avoid.

But: "Did you see the news?" I mumble. Apparently the self control I've been working on is wearing thin. "He bought another one."

Frankie hums. "I saw."

Of course she did. Frankie makes it her business to know about the biggest deals and acquisitions in the city. She likes knowing where the money's flowing. And for the last five days, Spencer Arnoult has been spending his fortune like a drunk man stumbling around Vegas.

Original artworks. More jewels. Literal gold. Apparently the tech billionaire has responded to his first break-in by building up his own dragon hoard.

"I don't like it." I stab at my third nail, splattering green polish all over my knuckle. "He'll attract the wrong attention. His security is not *that* great, obviously."

"Obviously."

"And I know I must have bruised his ego or whatever, but that doesn't mean he should overcompensate like this. He's tempting fate."

"He's certainly trying to tempt *someone*."

I shake my head hard, throat raw, because I can't let myself think that way. If he'd wanted me to stay, Spencer would have told me so, but instead he made that deal. He wanted my help, that was all.

And okay... maybe he wanted a few other things too. My face heats at the memory of his roaming hands, his possessive mouth, his darkly satisfied expression when he stared at me from between my legs.

But did he say anything about feelings? About *liking* me at all?

No. He did not.

I'm the girl who burgled him. Who scared him so badly he called the cops; who invaded his privacy and ate his leftovers. Who reneged on her promise to help with his security, and who pestered him like a crazy person for his touch.

He must have been so relieved to find me gone.

I know I would be.

* * *

Two days later, I'm moving into downward dog, my shoulders cracking and my ass high, when my phone buzzes from the floor beside my mat. Barely anyone has my personal number—only Frankie, and a couple more of our associates, and none of us call without good reason. Shit.

I topple to the side, hip banging against the floor. Spencer's right. I'm really not that graceful.

"Frankie?" Her name is lit up on my screen, but there's no sound coming down the line. It's like she's holding her breath. "Frankie? You okay?"

There's a grinding noise, like machinery getting stuck. That's her I'm-not-sure noise, but she's making it, so. That's a relief. I blow a stray lock of hair off my face and wait for her to arrange her thoughts.

They come out in a rush. "I did something bad. Maybe. I'm not sure if it was really bad, or just our regular kind of bad, you know? I, um. I hacked him. Spencer Arnoult. Again. I'm sorry. He redid all his cyber security, but I was curious about all the stuff he was buying and I wanted to make sure he wasn't, like, talking to the cops about you."

"He's not," I murmur. That's one thing I'm sure about. Even when he'd only known me for eight minutes, Spencer chose to look like an idiot instead of turn me in. "Don't read his stuff anymore, Frankie. We said we'd leave him alone."

"No, I know. Duh. And we will. But Spencer Arnoult left you a message."

I frown at my bare brick wall, heart thumping. That's not possible. There's no way.

"It must be for someone else."

Frankie scoffs. "Someone else called Tabitha? It was in his email drafts. Listen to this: *Tabitha, I know you've seen everything I'm buying. It's all for you. Come and get it—finders keepers.*"

Holy shit.

Am I having a heart attack? It kind of feels like a heart attack, but I barely even eat red meat. Is this a dream?

"*Ow.* Fuck." The pinch says no, this is very real. "What do I do?"

Lord knows why I'm asking Frankie of all people, but she starts talking louder, picking up speed. "He hasn't stored them all in his penthouse this time. They're scattered around the city. And he left you a map, and the locations are numbered, and I think you're supposed to—"

"Send it to me."

Frankie's affronted silence makes me grin so wide. "You're welcome, asshole. What am I, your P.A?"

"Thank you." I stand up with a groan, reaching down to roll my yoga mat, the phone pressed between my shoulder and my ear. "You're the best friend ever, and a superstar hacker. I'm so glad you called and if I can ever return the favor I will, and—"

"Alright, that's plenty." She blows out a heavy breath, the static crackling through the phone. "I just sent you everything. I can't believe you're in love, Tabby Cat. This is so weird."

It *is* weird, but if Frankie's noticed? It's also so obvious, I can no longer live in denial.

"Yep. It's weird and horrible and the best. Hopefully it happens to you soon."

She snorts and hangs up, and I toss my phone on the sofa then punch the air.

I need to squeal, to shower, and to dress all in black—in that order. I'm going on a treasure hunt.

Spencer

The map I left Tabitha was downloaded three hours ago. Three hours, since my phone pinged and my breathing stopped. That draft email sat there untouched for days, so long I nearly lost hope, and then out of nowhere... she's coming.

I *hope* she's coming, anyway. Fuck knows what I'll do if this doesn't work. Try to hire her for a job or something? Plaster love notes to her on billboards through the city?

Nothing's off the table. I don't care if everyone else thinks I've lost my mind. I need Tabitha.

Waking up with her gone was like waking up without a limb. Painful and horrifying and so disconcerting, I've barely managed to function. I haven't logged into my company emails for a week. I've been living off non-stop chicken satay noodles, like they'll somehow conjure her again. I've even kept that damn suitcase exactly where she left it in the hall.

Maybe it would hurt less if I hadn't seen her note. If I thought she was indifferent to me, and I could tell myself I was a fool for reading something into nothing. But there, in a looping script on a notepad on my desk, tucked beside my unlocked sapphire, were her words: *Spencer. I wish I could deserve you.*

Reading that note, I nearly tore my hair out. She does deserve me, whatever the fuck that means. And who cares, anyway? We love each other. We need each other. I know that, and surely she'll realize it soon too.

If she doesn't… well, I guess I'll keep trying. And maybe one day I'll find the right jewel to bring Tabitha home.

"All set, sir." I nod at the head of security at the city's finest hotel, striding past him into the empty vault. It cost a small fortune to rent their vault rather than a suite, and I know they all think I'm insane. Especially when I explained a woman would break in here tonight, and I'd be waiting for her.

It's the last number on her map. The end of the road—if she wants it to be.

"Thank you. And remember, don't go easy on her. Make her work for it."

The man nods, barely hiding his confusion. "Of course, sir."

She'll come. I tell myself that over and over as the vault door swings closed, plunging me into darkness. There's a pause, and then soft lights flicker on around the walls. It's plush in here. Like a high-security luxury elevator.

There's even a blue velvet cushioned chair in one corner, and a bottle of spring water. I guess that's why this hotel is the best.

I stride to the corner and take a seat, chest drumming.

Time to wait for my girl.

* * *

The second she bursts in, Tabitha is a blur, then she's in my lap. A red-faced security guard stares at us from the doorway, breathing hard, but when I jerk my chin at him, he closes the vault.

She's so warm. So *alive.* Trembling in my arms, dressed all in black like the night we met. I tug her beanie off, running my fingers through her caramel waves, shifting them to lay against her shoulders.

Warm silk. Fuck, I've missed her.

"You came," I rasp. "Thank you. I'm sorry, there's no treasure in this last one."

She gives a strangled laugh. "Yes there is."

I bury my face in the crook of her neck. Tabitha smells like green apple and sunshine, and I mumble against her heated skin, dragging my nose back and forth. "Did you buy the same shampoo as mine?"

"Yeah. I missed your smell."

I gather her closer, squeezing so hard that she squeaks.

"I got your note. It was bullshit, Tabitha."

"And I got yours. It was the best."

We sit like that for a while, sharing long, hungry breaths, so starved for each other's touch and warmth and presence. As her weight sinks into me, my pulse thuds harder in my cock. She's bundled on my lap, her shoeless feet dangling against my calf.

"I couldn't carry stuff with me. But, um, after I opened each vault, the security people arrived and offered to have it delivered to your penthouse for me."

Yeah, that was presumptuous. Wishful thinking on my part. I scowl at the wall, but I force the words out, because she found all those treasures fair and square. Finders keepers, I told her,

51

even if she doesn't want to keep *me*. "You can have them sent somewhere else if you prefer."

"No." A small hand finds mine. Links our fingers together. "No, I want to come home."

Yes. My chest cracks open, and sweet, cool relief floods over my raw insides. I can breathe again, finally, and it's because of Tabby. Because maybe she wants to keep me after all. I'm harder than ever, thrusting up against her without thinking, but I force myself to stop.

Not here. Not now.

I shudder out a sigh, pressing a long kiss to her forehead. "Thank god. I've eaten so much chicken satay, Tabitha."

* * *

I hold out until I get her in the backseat of the car. So much for delayed gratification—I can't go another fucking second without my hands on bare skin, her taste in my mouth, her sighs in my ear. It's been the longest week of my life.

"Tabby. Fuck." I throw a glance at the driver's partition, the opaque glass safely raised. I don't want anyone seeing her like this but me. She's scrambling into my lap, her knees scraping against the leather on either side of my hips, and her cheeks are pink with arousal. "I don't—I can't wait anymore."

What was I thinking, waiting the first time? I guess I assumed we'd have longer together. That I could tease her and torment her and drag it out until she was safely addicted to me too.

That did not go as planned.

"Me neither." She's rocking in my lap, pressing hungry kisses against my lips, my cheek, my jaw. Through the tinted windows, the late night traffic drifts slowly through the streets, and when she sucks a harsh bruise on my throat, I grunt.

She can mark me if she likes. Hell, she can tattoo 'Property of Tabitha' on my ass. It's true.

"Come here," I growl, grabbing her thighs and squeezing. Her black leggings are soft under my palms, and I stroke up and down her legs. Trace the seam over her core. I'm almost sorry when I tear the fabric down the center.

Almost.

But then Tabitha sucks in a shocked breath, and starts whining and rocking harder against my lap, and my fingertips creep inside the torn fabric. And she's damp and so hot, scorching through her blue panties, and when I pinch against her clit through the lace, she tips her head back with a groan.

"I'm not the only one who likes it mean. Am I, sweetheart?"

She shakes her head fast, the ends of her hair whipping my cheeks. "No. No, you're not."

Alright, then. I can do that for her. I can unleash this—this *edge* I feel when I'm around her, this brutal hunger, this sharpened side of my love. And fuck, I want to show her that side. I want us like this too: I want bared teeth and rough growls and grabbing hands.

She did this to me. I'm desperate.

"Shit." Tabitha yanks on my hair as I scrape my teeth down her throat. She grinds against my cock and I smack her ass hard. "What happened to the shy nerd?"

"You left him." I'm guttural. Ruined. "This is what's left, so tell me, Tabby. Do you still want me?"

"*Yes.*"

I don't play with her pussy. Don't want this to be gentle. Part of me still wants to punish her for leaving, and some instinct tells me she wants that too. So I grip her panties in my fist and twist them until she whimpers, squirming against my knuckles, and then I pull them to the side, reaching between us to draw out my length.

I'm flushed and ruddy. So hard it hurts.

I grip the back of her neck and give her a little shake. "Do it, sweetheart. Show you want me. Sit on my cock."

Tabitha

Spencer Arnoult is kind of unhinged. The sweet tease of last week is long gone, and in his place is a new man. His face is harsh, his teeth bared, and his grip on my neck is rough.

I love it.

Tingles race through my body as he manhandles me, urging me to kneel up and line up with his cock. Every nerve ending under my skin is sparking, and I'm so freaking alive right now. This is like scaling a building. Like cracking an impossible safe.

Danger, my instincts whisper. *Danger, danger.*

The thing is… I freaking love danger.

"Spencer." I nip the tip of his nose. "You've gone all caveman, and I love it, baby. Here, pull my hair." He huffs and wraps my hair around my fist, then grabs my hip and pushes me down onto his cock.

I'm wet, so slick and aching, but this is still my first time. It still *stings*, it burns like hell, and I'm only halfway down

Spencer's thick length before tears brim in my eyes and spill over onto my cheeks.

Shit. I can't breathe.

He freezes beneath me. The grip gentles on my hair, and then his low voice is so unsure. "…Tabitha? What's wrong? Don't you want this?"

I nod, smiling through my tears. I should have warned him. I know I should.

"I do! I do, I promise. Come on, I was practically begging you just now." He watches me, frowning. Not buying it. And god, if we don't do this right now, if I don't feel him *taking* me, owning me like that, being my caveman again, I'll die on the spot. "It's, uh. Okay, you're going to make me say it. I haven't—I've never—"

Realization dawns, and Spencer's forehead crashes against my shoulder. "Fuck. *Tabitha.* I was so rough with you just now."

"And I loved it." I roll my hips to demonstrate and okay, yeah, that feels better already. I just needed a minute, and now that burn has morphed into a delicious tickle. I hum, rocking harder, sliding him deeper inside me.

A stern hand grips my hip. "Don't force it. Don't hurt yourself."

Just for that, I sink further on his cock, hips twisting. "Don't boss me around, Arnoult." There's a pause, and then he growls and tugs on my hair again. Yeah, now we're talking.

"You're such a little brat."

"Uh-huh." I nod, rocking faster in his lap.

"Look at you, riding my cock like that. So needy and shameless." Yup. "You like it, Tabitha? You gonna stick around this time?" Spencer's eyes are hard and bright. He thrusts up beneath me, bouncing me on his length, and *lord*, I hope his cruel grip on my thigh leaves bruises. I want to collect them with my other pretty things.

But Spencer doesn't even notice the way he's squeezing me. The way his thrusts knock the air from me every time. He's gazing into my eyes, bleak and tortured.

"Don't leave me again, Tabitha. You hear me? Swear it." A rough hand finds my breast through my black top, kneading and squeezing. "I'll buy whatever jewels you want. Hide them behind the best security. Just don't fucking go."

"I won't." My fingers weave into his dark hair, and I hang on for dear life. "I won't, I promise." I grind down, taking his whole length inside me, and gasp up at the car ceiling, seeing stars.

It's fucked up. I know it; he knows it. We're a twisted, messed up pair, and whatever is between us isn't normal. Probably isn't healthy.

But I also know that I've never felt safer. More loved or secure. More *wanted*, coveted like the finest treasure—and I've never wanted a person the way I want Spencer Arnoult.

I'd trade all my stolen goods for him. Every pretty thing I've ever owned. They're nothing compared to the vivid green of his eyes.

Spencer reaches between us and pinches my clit again, laughing darkly when I moan. He spanks me there, too, and every tiny hit is a red-hot cascade of sensation. The air in the backseat is hot, muggy with the smell of sex, and condensation creeps over the tinted windows.

Leather creaks. Traffic drifts past the window.

I slam down on his cock, trying to take all of him every single time. And all at once Spencer lets go, spreading his arms out along the seat backs, and he looks so dangerous and arrogant that I nearly come right there.

"Keep going."

I suck in a ragged breath, rocking and grinding. He feels so fucking good, filling me up until I'm not hollow at all. I pluck at my nipples through my top, teasing him, and his eyes narrow. "Nice try. You're going to come without my hands on you, Tabitha. Call it an incentive. Something you'll have to stick around for."

Maybe we need to play these games. Maybe he needs the reassurance that I'll stay.

Maybe it's just fun. Enjoyably messed up.

"Please," I beg, because I'm so in. I love our games. "Touch me, Spencer."

"No."

The trembles start in my legs. They travel through my whole body, flushing me hot, filling me with a thousand burning sparks. I clamp down on Spencer's cock with a groan, twisting my hips, corkscrewing him deeper. Dimly, beyond my ragged breaths and ringing ears, I feel him swell up then spill inside me. He sounds as ruined as I feel.

I come down slowly, settling back in my body. I'm all sticky and sleepy.

My jaw cracks as I yawn.

"Okay, sweetheart." Spencer helps me off his lap, cleaning me up with a tissue he magics up from somewhere in the car, and he's so achingly gentle now. My lovely nerd isn't gone for good, then. "You did so well."

He buckles me in and presses a kiss on my forehead. "We're nearly home."

"My leggings," I mumble, and he huffs out a laugh.

"We'll wrap my jacket around your waist. Sorry about that."

I'm not. It was so freaking hot, and who cares? I have dozens of pairs of black leggings.

"You can make it up to me later," I tell him, though, because I'm still the same person. A shameless opportunist who loves tricks and deals.

It doesn't matter. This man loves me just as I am.

Spencer

❦

hree years later

There's someone in my office. It's late, I'm on the top floor of the company building, and I should be the only person here, all alone with the stars winking through the windows and traffic snaking past far below. My assistant left hours ago, leaving me to the scheduled meeting with the Singapore team, and I should be alone, yet the hairs have risen on the back of my neck.

"Tabby?" I call, my voice bouncing through the empty office. I frown at the shadows near the elevator. "Tabitha?"

Nothing.

I shiver.

It's nothing new for me to feel like I'm being watched at work, and I _know_ my assistant didn't steal all those company pens, damn it. My wife loves pranks and she can't help her sticky fingers, but since Tabby hit her second trimester, I thought maybe she'd slow down.

Cool hands wrap around my eyes from behind. "Gotcha."

Guess not.

I blow out a hard breath. "If you came up the elevator shaft in your condition, I swear to god—"

"Don't be ridiculous." Warm lips skate over my neck. "I'm not an idiot. I took the stairs."

"*Tabby*. We're on the top floor."

Her clothes rustle, and I can feel her shrug. "You like these thighs, don't you? They don't come from nothing, Arnoult."

Yeah, okay. I do love those thighs, so much that even the mention of them makes me hot under the collar. I flick my top button undone, glancing at my watch. Eight minutes until the Singapore meeting.

A lot can happen in eight minutes.

"Get up on my desk. Just—carefully, damn it." I turn and watch Tabitha stroll away, lifting herself easily onto the polished wood like she's not carrying a whole other life in there. "Spread your legs. Yeah."

Her blue eyes sparkle as I prowl closer. No matter how much of my inner animal I let out, Tabitha meets me on that level. She urges me on, begs me to go harder. Fuck, I love her so much.

She's all in black again. Of course she is. It makes her caramel hair sparkle.

"You gonna tear another pair of my leggings, Arnoult?"

I grin, heart pounding. She makes me so savage. "Why? Have you been hiding spares in my drawer again?"

Tabby smirks. Yeah, I found them this morning.

I take two handfuls of black cotton and rip, and her throaty laugh fills my chest like molten gold.

"I have a meeting soon." I grip the back of her neck, grinning as she sighs.

"I know. I'm all about timing."

"Well, tough shit. I'm going to lick you out, going to make you beg, and you won't get the rest until I get back tonight."

Tabitha pouts, plays the brat and tosses her hair, but she loves it like this. Even after three years and two rings on our fingers, we both like the reassurance that the other's coming home.

"You're lucky I love you," Tabby grumbles as she lays back on my desk, and she's teasing, but I'm not going to argue.

I know.

I'm the luckiest man in the world.

II

Hacker

Description

I've watched the mobster from afar for years.

But he finds out he's been hacked–and now he's coming for me.

This city is my home, and my best entertainment. Who needs TV when I've got this freak show at my fingertips?

I like to know everything–all the schemes, the threats, the betrayals. Usually, I kick back and watch it unfold with popcorn, but when it's *him* in danger, I can't resist.

I send a warning. My weird little crush demands it. And though it saves the mobster... well, he's not exactly grateful.

He sends his own warning. He's going to find me, and then he'll kill me.

…Honestly.

Is it really so hard to say thank you?

Frankie

Whenever I need to make a big decision, I have three different plans of attack. Option one: call my friend Tabitha to check what a normal person would do—and hopefully get her boyfriend Spencer to weigh in, since as a cat burglar, she's not that normal either.

Option two: draw on the collective wisdom of the internet, and hope my exact predicament has come up before. This is good for laundry questions and houseplant care; not so much for illegal activities.

Or option three: roll my favorite dice and hope for the best.

I lean back in my desk chair and frown at the spread of computer screens, blue light washing over me in a sickly glow. It's late, but that's okay. That's not why my brain's stuck. I'm a night owl, and I think better after midnight.

The handful of dice dig into my palm as I squeeze them tight, and I rap twice on the desk with my stuffed hand. I can't tear my eyes away from the screens; can't even blink.

Luca Bianchi will die tonight.

Oh, he's got a few hours left in him. The literal backstabbing is set for 5am, after which point the mobster will be nothing but a pile of dead limbs and a red puddle on the floor. Is he having a good night, at least? Did he have a delicious last meal? What did he eat?

It took me a long time to unearth this plan, digging through private servers and coded communications, and honestly, I stumbled onto it by chance. Luca's cousin has been careful. I doubt even the kingpin will realize it was him—that the hit came from inside the house.

But *I'll* know. I found that weasel's breadcrumb trail and followed it all the way back to an assassin. He's taken out a hit on his own cousin, and for what? The chance to take over Luca's activities, probably. To become the new spymaster.

Dude. That's not how it works. If someone had me killed, they wouldn't magically become a great hacker, and he won't inherit Luca's web of secrets and intrigue. It'll just disappear. Evaporate in a puff of smoke. Such a waste.

Because Luca is *good.* A genius, really. That's why I like him so much—or part of it, anyway. As a rule, I don't lie to myself, so I'll also admit that the thick bronze hair, square jaw and moss green eyes don't hurt either.

We're all animals deep down, even me, and I exist more online than in the real world.

And my inner animal *really* likes Luca Bianchi.

"Shit."

I grab my phone, then sigh and toss it on the desk. Pick it up, then put it down. What good would calling Tabitha do? She doesn't know Luca like I do. She hasn't watched him for months, *years*, like he's her favorite TV show. She's not properly invested. She doesn't have all the facts.

I think Tabitha would tell me to stay out of mob business. So I'm not gonna call her.

And there's no point checking online. Somehow I doubt there's a forum for this.

Okay, so that leaves my trusty dice. An odd number, and I'll warn him. Even, and I won't. I'll let Luca Bianchi die.

The dice clatter over my desk, the sound cutting over the soft music pulsing from the speakers I've got hooked on all the walls. Most of them land in a neat halo, but one bounces off the keyboard at a weird angle and drops onto the floorboards below. I scowl, but count up all the other dice first.

Nineteen so far. An odd number. That's good.

My legs are stiff as I climb out of my desk chair, my ass sore from hours on the plush leather. The chair almost cost more than my screens, but I still feel like an old woman every time I get up after too long in one position.

I can't help it. My focus snags on something, then I get absorbed. Like on Luca Bianchi for instance—I've got more than one dead leg after staring at his stuff for hours. Reading his emails; scrolling through his bank accounts, both legitimate and hidden. Scanning his appointments and trying to decode his private notes.

He makes it hard for me, not like most of the power players in this city. I like that.

One time I hacked his laptop webcam and watched a live feed of his kitchen for four hours. He made tortellini from scratch and called to threaten an informant while stirring the sauce. And later on, he wandered past the doorway shirtless on his way to the shower.

That was such a good night.

It's dark under the desk, away from the screens. It takes a

second for my eyes to adjust, then I spot the ghostly white cube beside the table leg. My mouth goes dry.

Three.

I stare at the three dots, plucking the die off the floorboards. It brings a tiny clump of dust.

So: twenty two. An even number, which means I won't warn him.

Decision made. I'll let Luca Bianchi die.

* * *

Okay, forget that. How do you even tell a person they're about to be betrayed? I don't like sending the simplest messages. I can't do small talk, and everyday interactions confound me. This is way above my pay grade.

And even if I figure out the wording, how do I do it? How do I get in touch? Ideally, I'd leave an anonymous note on his computer or something. Let him find it in his own time, and erase any trace of me so he can't figure out who sent it. But I'm on the clock here, and there's a chance Luca is asleep, so I need to get his attention fast.

My brain's whirring so much, I need a fan in my skull. I lunge to my feet, stumbling to my kitchen on wobbly legs. When did I last eat?

A bowl of curry instant noodles and a sickly sweet energy drink later, I collapse back into my chair, breathing hard. *Focus, Frankie.*

The stakes are high on this one. Stupid dice don't know what they're talking about. Luca Bianchi is *not* a man I can sit back and watch die... but he's not someone whose attention I want, either. He got pissed off last month when a neighbor

70

signed for a package for him. He's a very private, territorial person. A dangerous man.

He won't take well to discovering he's been hacked.

A glance at the clock makes sweat break out on my palms. It's past 3am. Time's running out for Luca.

"Crap. Double crap. Oh shit. Oh shit."

I got into his phones months ago. He's got three of them: one for business, one for family-personal, and one for *actual*-personal. He barely uses that one, but I think he likes the idea of having private space.

That's the phone I go into now, my fingers flying over the keyboard. I set an appointment in the calendar: *Get murdered* at 5am, then set a loud reminder to chime out until he swipes it off.

Is that enough? How will I know if he's seen it? I stare at the potted ivy vines trailing down the wall beside my desk, my eyes dry and heart pounding.

I should be sure. This is Luca Bianchi. I should be extra certain.

So I set a dozen more appointments and alerts on every piece of Luca Bianchi's tech that I've ever hacked. All his phones and his laptop. His smart watch and tablet. If he lives long enough to get in his car again, his sat nav will warn him too.

Then I dial everything up to maximum volume, sit back in my chair, and let them chime.

Luca

Someone is fucking with me, which means that someone is going to die. This was already a shitty, waste-of-breath day, with one of my best moles in the police department caught stealing documents, and my favorite cooking show getting axed. I'm not in the fucking mood.

The first alert comes from my personal phone. My *really* personal phone. I've barely snatched it up from my nightstand and silenced the alarm before the others start to ring out.

All of them.

My laptop pings rhythmically from the kitchen counter, loud enough for the sound to float through the wall. All of my phones are chiming now, the volume dialed up even louder, and even my smart watch flashes and vibrates on the bureau.

What. The. Fuck.

Do I seem like the kind of man it would be fun to prank? Have I let myself appear soft? It's true that I don't relish violence the way some in the mob do, but that's a matter of personal taste. Not fear.

Whoever is doing this will die. Painfully. I will make an example of them.

Because this is my *space*. My territory. These are my fucking things. Whoever is doing this has clearly hacked all my tech, and for what? A stupid wake up call? Making me lose a few hours of sleep?

I swipe off another alert, then my tired eyes snag on the text. I've been glancing at the reminders, seeing without really reading, but my sleep-fogged brain is finally catching up.

The alerts all say the same thing: *Get murdered,* 5am.

Huh.

Well, if it's a prank, I guess it's slightly better. More unsettling. And if it's not… who the fuck would warn me like this? Everyone I know would call, or meet in person. Not hack my smart watch and personal phone.

It's still an invasion. Even if they're right, they'll pay. I dig the heels of my palms into my eyes, mind whirring as I plot out scenarios.

Who would want me dead?

Lots of people.

But who would have the guts to try it?

Not so many.

5am is not far away. I need a plan now.

My jaw cracks as I yawn, shaking my head and striding toward the shower, my personal phone gripped in one hand and a switchblade in the other. Will I die in the next ten minutes? Unlikely. But the water will wake me up, will get a solution out of me, and besides…

I'm not meeting my maker in fucking pajama pants.

* * *

I stand outside a warehouse on the city docks, arms folded and a salty breeze tugging at my hair. Dawn's breaking, the horizon a burning red line, and waves slosh against the stone dock walls.

"This is bullshit." My cousin Sal stands at my side, arms crossed, his posture matching mine. Sal's always copied me, even when we were boys, and right now we've even got matching dark shadows under our eyes. "He came to your apartment? That's personal, Luca."

No shit. Aren't all assassination attempts pretty personal when it comes down to it?

I frown at the oil drum perched on the dock's edge. Two lower-downs are stuffing bricks through the hole, weighing it down, because the last thing I want is my hit man floating out to sea, bobbing around in the shipping lane.

"How'd you know he was coming?" Sal prods, and the hairs prickle on my neck. I shoot a glance at my cousin, but he's not watching. He's gesturing at our helpers, making them stuff the barrel quicker. The light's coming up fast, and we've all got shit to do today.

I only called him because he's head of clean up. Figured it would make this all go faster.

Now I'm wondering if Sal and I should have a chat.

"I always know."

Not true, but he doesn't need to hear that. A big part of my role is the mystique—people spew out their secrets faster when they think it's inevitable either way. Sal's always been jealous of my job; has always resented playing clean up. It's a vital task, but he thinks it's degrading. Following around after the big boys.

"I'll know about the next one, too. And I'll figure out who's sending them, no problem."

Sal shifts his weight, sweat beading on his thinning hairline. He still won't look at me. My eyes narrow.

"What do you think I'll do to them, Sal? When I figure out who wants me dead?" My voice is soft, but I don't need to yell to get my message across. And sure enough, when my cousin shrugs, the movement's jerky.

"You'll wipe 'em out, Luca."

"'Course I will."

A hunch isn't proof. I won't kill a cousin on a hunch, and not in broad daylight right next to the last body I made. It's sloppy, and besides, the boss wouldn't be happy.

But a hunch can become proof, and if I'm right about Sal, he won't be breathing for very much longer. I might pity him—he's always been so tragic, with his droopy jowls and the whine to his voice—but that fucking hit man knocked my espresso maker off the kitchen counter. I loved that thing. I imported it from Milan.

My cousin jolts when I clap a hand on his shoulder, giving him a friendly squeeze. "You should take the day off, Sal. You seem stressed."

We watch as our helpers shove the barrel over the wall's edge, the metal grating over the rough stone. There's a loud splash, the rush of bubbles... then nothing. I'm still gripping Sal's shoulder. He wants to shake me off, but he won't.

"I'm fine," he says. "I'm fine."

The choppy waves glint like steel in the rising sunlight.

"I need a trace," I tell Sal, because he won't know how to piece this together anyway. The knowledge won't do him any good, even if my hunch is right. "IP address, phone number, social security. The whole deal. Send Alessandro to my place for eight."

He sighs. "Sure, Luca." He looks older already, but hey, *I* didn't age him. He chose this nonsense. "You need a clean up crew at your apartment too?"

"Just my regular lady." I already bleached all the blood and dealt with the signs of foul play. My normal cleaner Ola can handle the rest.

She's discreet. Trustworthy, unlike some pieces of shit. And I really need one of her perogies today.

It's barely dawn, and I'm already sinking bodies at the docks. Someone hacked my fucking sat nav, and my espresso machine broke. Sometimes I think this life is not worth it, and those thoughts are crowding in fast this morning.

I push them all away. No time to brood just yet.

There's still one problem gnawing at my brain. I've got a hacker to hunt.

Frankie

I fling a backpack onto my unmade bed, tugging the zips open and standing back with a huff. What do people pack when they run for their lives? Would *that* question be on an internet forum? I gaze around my messy bedroom, dazed and lost.

Luca Bianchi lived past 5am. I watched the fight through his laptop webcam on the kitchen counter, my heart in my mouth and my nails digging into my palms. Luca's a tall man, packed with lean muscle, but the hit man was *big*. A heavy-boned bruiser. I stood there and wished Luca wasn't so freaking stubborn, that he'd just disappeared and left an empty apartment for the hit man to find.

There was no sound through the webcam, but I flinched when the espresso machine hit the floor, shards of metal flying across the tiles. Luca loved that thing. He's going to be extra pissy, and if he finds me, he'll take it out on me.

The sat nav was overkill. An extra insult. I know that now, but I can't turn back time, can I?

I don't regret warning him either, even if it means I'm screwed now. I've never felt relief like seeing that hit man go down. Luca didn't drag it out or make it messy, and I like that about him. He doesn't relish gore like some men in his position. He's efficient. He gets the job done, and then he moves on.

If he finds me, will he kill me quickly too?

Oh my god. I need to get out of here. *Focus, Frankie.*

This is a bad time to have an easily-distracted brain. More than ever, I need to focus on one task at a time and not fixate on Luca Bianchi and his plump lips. Those thick, sooty eyelashes that would be feminine on another man. He could be a model, sure, but that doesn't mean I should stand here and daydream about him until he turns up and shoots me dead.

Would he do that? A gun doesn't seem like his style.

Shit. Double shit.

My movements sluggish, I force myself to pack while my skittish thoughts circle round and round in my head. I shove my passport, wallet, keys, dice, and a stack of emergency cash into my backpack. Then a spare tank top and three pairs of plain white cotton underwear.

A hairbrush.

Deodorant.

Toothbrush, toothpaste and soap.

Oh my god, do I need a weapon? If Luca turned up here, could I even concentrate enough to use one? What else should I take?

Hell. I am not equipped for this. I got carried away with my fixation on Luca Bianchi, and now I'm in uncharted territory with no map. Stupid crush.

Digging through my bedroom drawers, I find my grimy

old pocket knife, then add the half empty plastic lighter I use to light my apple scented candles. It's the saddest weaponry you've ever seen, but it's all I've got. I'm a hacker, not a fighter, and it's not like the kitchen's kitted out. I *never* cook. I don't even own a cheese grater.

Running to the cupboards, I toss three packets of instant noodles into my backpack and zip it shut. Gotta go, gotta go. Every second, the risk gets greater of Luca finding me. I'm clattering across my living room, yanking the backpack onto my shoulders, when my phone buzzes in my pocket.

I freeze, heart pounding. Then lie to myself, just for a second.

Maybe it's Tabitha, or one of the other girls. Maybe it's a spam call.

I draw my phone out, fingers shaking. Why do I answer? Maybe some tragic, needy part of me wants to hear his voice.

"Hello, Francine." It's deep and warm in my ear. Like we're old friends catching up, but an old friend wouldn't call me that.

I lick my dry lips. "Actually, it's Frankie."

"Frankie," he repeats, his tone still warm. Like we're meeting over breakfast. Like he wants to reach through the phone and shake my hand. "You did a hell of a job on my tech, Frankie. Apparently if you hadn't announced yourself like that, I might never have known you were there."

Ah, yeah. There's the anger I expected. The bite to his words.

"Sorry about your espresso machine," I whisper.

A beat of silence. Then: "You watched what happened."

I don't answer, because I don't need to. Luca already knows.

"Do you watch me often, Frankie?" He sounds irritated, but curious too. The mobster wants to figure me out, wants to make sense of me before he swats me like a gnat.

"Sometimes." The word comes out all gravelly, so I clear my throat. "I like watching you cook. All I eat is instant noodles."

There's a soft laugh, and all the tiny hairs on my body stand on end. It's a menacing laugh, and I should *not* get so flushed and tingly over it.

"That's an invasion of my privacy, Frankie."

I wrinkle my nose. "I know."

What am I supposed to say? I'm a hacker. All I do is invade people's privacy, and I figured Luca Bianchi of all people would understand that.

People like us, we deal in secrets. It's our main currency, but apparently it's only okay for him to do it, or for it to happen to other people. *Men.*

"I'm hanging up now," I tell him, because I need to end this call. If he knows my number, he probably knows my address too. This conversation is a distraction, a way for him to buy time. "If you don't cause me any trouble, I won't hurt you either."

It's not an empty threat. I've got months' worth of material on this guy, and he has zero regard for the law. I could give Luca Bianchi one hell of a headache... if I lived long enough, anyway.

There's a slow inhale, then a gust of breath. I inch toward my front door, rummaging in my newly stuffed bag for my key. Why did I throw it in there first, then pile a load of crap on top? I suck at this.

"It's a pity," Luca says quietly, like he's talking to himself. "I could have used your skills, Frankie. I would have paid well for them, too. But the insult can't stand."

Got it! I jab the key in the lock, twisting it as one of my instant noodles packets slips out of my bag onto the floor. I kick it behind me in a rustle of plastic.

I always lock myself in when I'm at home, because I live in a fancy building with a bunch of rich men. I don't trust a single one of them, and I *know* they all hate me. I scruff up the elevator with my sweatpants and battered sneakers.

That's one of the reasons I chose this building. I like pissing them off. It's funny.

The door swings open, and I sigh with relief at the empty hallway with its cream walls and potted palms. He should have come here quicker. It's not like him to make mistakes.

"Bye, Luca."

"Wait—"

"I'm glad you're not dead. Don't trust your cousin Salvatore." I hang up, bring up the call record, dig a pen out of my bag, and scrawl Luca's phone number on the back of my hand in messy blue ink. I vaguely recognize it: he's calling from his actually-personal cell. Didn't even block the number. Is he being sloppy, or does he want me to have it?

Doesn't matter. I toss my phone back into the apartment, slam the door and spin the key in the lock. I can go to ground for a few days. Figure things out.

Before long, Luca Bianchi will forget all about me.

If I don't call him, anyway.

Luca

My hacker lives in one of the most expensive buildings in the city, in a two-bedroom apartment with a large balcony. If I wanted proof that she's skilled, here it is, because places like this take a lot of money. And if I wanted proof that she's unhinged, here that is too.

Because her apartment is wild. *Literally* wild, like one of those photos of nature reclaiming abandoned buildings. Every surface is covered with clusters of potted plants; everywhere I look are waxy green leaves and trailing vines. There are so many plants in her apartment, the air feels different from the hallway. More humid. Every room smells faintly of damp soil.

Running and leaving these plants behind must have hurt her. She's clearly attached, in a strange way. So she'll be back. I'm counting on it.

I shouldn't have called Frankie like that. It gave her too much warning, it let her escape, and I don't even know why I rushed into it. I was so impatient to speak with her. But it was a long morning, so I'll forgive myself for the lapse in judgment, because it's not like she can hide from me forever.

Within hours of her alarms, I knew every single thing about her. Now I know her name and date of birth—and the fact that at twenty two, she's too young for me. I know where her estranged parents live. I've felt the clothes in her closet and sniffed the food in her fridge.

Frankie didn't lie when she told me she lives off instant noodles. It's disgusting. If I let her live, I'm going to force feed her vegetables.

Fidgeting with my personal phone, I stand on her balcony with the breeze playing over my cheeks. She hasn't called yet. Will she call? Probably not, since I threatened to kill her. The lights of the city glow under the stars, and I lean my elbows on the railing with a sigh.

I've been here all day, except for a few meetings in the afternoon. Don't want to go back to my own place. What's there for me, anyway? A broken espresso machine and the violation of being hacked; empty rooms and the lingering tang of bleach.

Sal might try again tonight. Put out another hit. I would if I were him, because his situation is now truly desperate. But even if he does, I won't be there. No one knows where I am.

"Come on, Frankie." I drum my fingers on the railing, jaw tight. I want to nip this situation in the bud, that's all. It's not about hearing her raspy voice again.

Though she called me Luca, not Mr Bianchi. Like she really knows me. And no one ever sees me cooking, so I guess in a way she does.

The buzzing phone takes a weight off my shoulders. I answer quickly, pressing the handset to my ear, and ignore the rioting sensation behind my rib cage.

"Good evening, Frankie."

There's a long pause. I wait, breath held.

Then, quiet as the breeze: "Hi, Luca."

All at once, the tension bleeds from my limbs. I roll my stiff neck, gazing down at the city lights, wondering which glowing golden square is hiding my hacker. "I wasn't sure you'd call."

"It's a burner," she says quickly, like I'm tracing her location. I probably should, but I'm not. "By the time you get here, I'll be long gone."

I tug at my collar, flicking the top button open. Relaxing at last. "I won't bother, then."

"Oh," Frankie says. "Um. Good."

"Where are you staying?" I'm not expecting an address or anything. She's a smart girl, and I clearly can't be trusted, but I'd like some visual details. Something to help me picture her.

The color of the walls, maybe, or what she dresses in to sleep. The precise shade of her dark hair. The security footage from this building was too grainy, though even those fuzzy images of her were enough to make my throat dry. "Do you have somewhere safe for the night?"

Frankie snorts. My lips twitch. Yes, it's a ridiculous question.

"I'm staying with a friend."

Teeth gritted, I tamp down the hot rush of jealousy. "I see." The pause stretches between us, until I can't help myself. I need to ask. "A platonic friend?"

Frankie's laugh is real now. Brassy and delighted. "You're jealous," she crows, and I smirk out at the rooftops. Her amusement is contagious. "If you wanted me to spend the night alone, you shouldn't have chased me from my apartment, Luca."

The smile drops off my face. "I *do* want you to spend the night alone."

"Well, like I said." She's more serious now too. "I'm staying with a friend."

"Another hacker?" Do they travel in packs? Have underground professional conferences? Is it a man?

"No," Frankie murmurs. "You'd like her, though. She deals in information too, but she tricks it out of people in person. Flirts with them until they blab all their secrets."

She doesn't offer any more details, and I don't ask. Useful or not, I don't care about Frankie's honey trap friend. Only the raspy girl on the phone.

"It is platonic," she blurts when I don't say anything more. "It's not—it's nothing like that."

Relief settles over me, cool and soothing like the first drops of rain. I peer up at the dark clouds gathering, blocking the stars.

"You should come back here. Water your plants." How long will they survive with her gone? It would be a shame for her to return to a wasteland. "Maybe I won't kill you after all."

Her soft puff of laughter makes my chest squeeze. "Such a great offer, Luca. Thank you." You can hear the smile in her voice.

"You're welcome," I tell her. "Think it over."

When the line goes dead, I slide the phone back into my pocket. The rain's coming down faster now, soaking through my shirt and suit jacket, clinging to my hair, but I don't go back inside. I stand out on the balcony and breathe in the scent of wind and wet stone, and feel the cold moisture seep through to my skin.

This silence after talking to Frankie, this emptiness in my

chest… it feels like loss.

I need my hacker to call me again.

* * *

I do get a call, but not the one I want. It comes through to my family-personal cell a little after ten, and I roll my eyes before answering. I'm stretched out on Frankie's sofa, a bag of microwave popcorn burning my hip. Trashy, but after a handful, I do see the appeal. "Yes?"

"Luca," Sal greets me. "Cousin, where are you tonight? Want to get a drink?"

He sounds nervous. He should be. More than anything, he wants to keep his distance from me—all of his survival instincts are screaming at him to stay away. But he needs me gone before I get concrete proof of what he's done, and that means luring me out.

Sal doesn't know about Frankie's warning. Paired with my earlier hunch, that's confirmation enough for me.

I flip over the paperback I stole off Frankie's nightstand to glance at the front again. It's a fantasy novel, with a mob of orcs and elves and practically nude busty women on the cover. "I'm reading."

Sal chuckles. "Uh. Where?"

"Does it matter?" I turn a yellowed page with my thumb. "It's a one-man job."

"Right." Sal's breaths are shaky. This much stress is bad at his age. "So you don't want a drink? I'm buying."

I grin, my expression savage though there's no one around to see. "There's a first time for everything, huh?"

Sal forces a laugh, and you know, I don't think this is purely about the role. He doesn't just hate being the cleaner. This guy really hates my guts. My own blood.

It's a kick in the teeth. He's a few years older, but I saved his ass from getting kicked all through growing up. Should've let them stamp my slimy cousin into the ground.

"So you'll meet me at Vinny's?"

I rummage in the popcorn bag. "Tomorrow, maybe."

Sal wants me dead by tomorrow, but hey—life is cruel. We can't always get what we want. For instance, I want a certain hacker girl balanced on my thighs. I want her raspy voice in my ear, begging me to touch her. And I want more of Ola's perogies, and for everyone to stop fucking calling me. Everyone except Frankie.

"Sure, maybe," Sal says, playing it cool because he knows he's pushing too hard. This guy wants to gather secrets? Please. He's as subtle as a brick. "I'll see you at the boss's in the morning."

He hangs up quickly so he's first. Such a child. I toss the phone onto Frankie's striped Moroccan rug, then find my place in her book again.

My hacker reads some smutty stuff, that's for sure.

I turn another page, eyebrows raised.

Frankie

Luca Bianchi has made himself at home in my apartment. I don't know what I expected when I borrowed a laptop to log into my home security system, but it definitely wasn't the world's best dressed squatter, striding from room to room in his tailored gray suit.

I figured Luca might smash up my things. The computers, at the very least.

Then I figured he'd leave me the rubble there as a warning to stay out of his business.

Instead, after spending the night on my sofa, Luca's in my kitchen digging through the cupboards. I don't have sound so I can't hear what he's muttering, but from his jerky movements and the way his lips keep moving, I'm pretty sure he's cursing me out.

It's true, my kitchen is tragic. I never bothered to buy more than a single saucepan and a wooden spoon. A few plates and bowls and forks and shit came with the place, but mostly I eat my noodles out of mugs.

"He's still there?"

A soft voice cuts through the quiet. My friend June places a steaming peppermint tea at my elbow, then settles at the kitchen table beside me. She sips from her own drink, her delicate eyebrows pinched in a frown, staring at Luca on the screen.

I shrug, my neck stiff from a night on June's sofa. Her apartment is smaller than mine, all strangely shaped rooms and bright walls and streaming sunlight. Her wrought iron balcony overlooks the arts district.

It's a nice place. I'm lucky to stay here, even if there are hardly any plants.

But watching Luca rummage through my kitchen cupboards is giving me this weird rush of homesickness. And when I turn to June, I can't help noticing that she and Luca share the same thick, bronze hair; the same smooth, tan skin.

I always knew June was pretty. But now I get why men fall over themselves to tell her their dirty secrets.

If Luca Bianchi flashed me his dimples, I'd probably write down all my passwords. And if he flirted with me? Forget it. I'd be putty in his hands.

"What's he looking for?" June tilts her head, watching him over the rim of her mug. Out of nowhere, I get the impulse to clap my hand over her eyes and stop her looking, because Luca's taken off his suit jacket and rolled his white shirt to the elbows. His gray pants hug his toned ass and thighs, and god, he's perfect. I don't want anyone else to see the shift of muscles under his clothes.

"Cooking equipment, probably." I take a sip of peppermint tea to soothe my tight throat. "I don't have any."

June huffs a laugh, nudging me with her elbow. "I could

teach you to cook, you know, Frankie."

"I know." So could the internet. So could the back of food packets. But it just doesn't interest me—not unless it's Luca Bianchi doing it. Honestly, he could sit there tying and untying his shoelaces and I'd probably be transfixed, watching his clever fingers and the flex of muscle in his broad shoulders.

Right now, he's glaring at my sparse cupboards, his hands propped on his narrow hips. Biting my lip, I pull another burner phone from my pocket. It's a new one, just in case he tracked last night's. Somehow, I don't think he did.

The number scrawled on the back of my hand nearly washed off in the shower. I went over it this morning in permanent marker.

The phone rings once before Luca answers, whipping his cell from his pocket and pressing it to his ear. He's still glaring at my cupboards. "Frankie?"

"Yeah." On the screen, his shoulders relax an inch. "Um, hi. Good morning. There are pop tarts on the second shelf if you're hungry."

Luca stiffens again, his body going rigid on the screen, then he wheels around, accusing mossy eyes searching for the camera.

That's the thing about plants. They draw the eye. You can fill an apartment with vines and leaves and flowers, and that's all anyone will see. Never the tiny black lenses peeking between the foliage.

"You're watching me again, Frankie." Luca's voice is rougher in the morning, but he doesn't sound mad. He sounds pleased. "Invading my privacy."

Hardly. "You're in *my* apartment. I'm not even hacking anything, I just logged into my own system."

"Did you watch me all night?" Luca presses. He rubs a hand over his jaw absentmindedly as he talks, and I can almost hear the rasp of stubble. What would that feel like under my fingertips? Or chafing against my skin? Does he *want* me to have watched him?

"Not all night," I lie.

Luca raises an eyebrow, still scanning for the camera. Behind him, the kitchen is a riot of clean dishes left stacked haphazardly on the draining board; wild, rangy plants; and buttery sunshine filtering through the open window.

"You ate my popcorn. And you read my book."

I see the exact moment Luca spots the camera tucked on a shelf between two spider plants. The frown melts from his handsome face, and his smirk… it makes my toes curl.

"Oh, my," June murmurs, fanning herself. Shit, I forgot she was here. I spin the laptop screen away from her, shrugging when she snorts and rises to leave.

I'm being petty and ungrateful. I know that, I do.

But I do *not* want my friend drooling over Luca Bianchi. He's mine.

"Is someone else there?" My mobster is frowning again.

"It's just my friend June. She's gone into another room."

Luca stays silent and thoughtful, and I miss that smirk so badly it hurts. And though I could happily stay on the line to this man for hours, I won't kid myself that he'd want that. I need to make this call worth his while.

"Did you check out your cousin Salvatore?"

Luca grunts, then turns to find the pop tarts, probing one-handed at the shelf. "Yes. He is suddenly very interested in my whereabouts."

I bet. Luca's cousin must feel like he's on a timer, the seconds ticking down as he gets more and more desperate. "Don't tell him where you are."

"Worried about your plants?" Luca asks lightly. He's found the pop tart box. He fishes out a chocolate one and drops it in the toaster.

"No." My stomach cramps, but it's not hunger. It's fear. "I'm worried about you, obviously. Why do you think I warned you the first time? I knew it would screw up my life."

Luca's quiet at that. The air shimmers above the toaster from the heat.

Finally, he says, "I am not an easy man to kill."

No kidding.

If he was more normal, more *mortal*, maybe I would have more things to say right now. Or maybe I'd have gone home already, and we could be eating pop tarts together.

But Luca Bianchi is not a friendly house guest. He's a mobster, and he promised to kill me. Even if he's decided to let me live, that doesn't mean he wants to hang out and eat breakfast. Why am I kidding myself about this?

"Frankie?" Luca sounds cautious. Like he can sense my drop in mood through the phone. "Are you still there?"

His chocolate pop tart jolts in the toaster. I squeeze my burner phone, palm clammy.

"Your breakfast is ready."

"Well, I'd hardly call this food."

"Have a good day, Luca. Don't meet up with your cousin."

"Wait, Frankie—"

I hang up on him, breathing fast. On the screen, Luca stares at his phone, jaw clenched, his chest rising and falling under his shirt. For a moment, I think he might smash his cell. Might toss it against the wall and shower my kitchen tiles with glass.

That's what mobsters do, right? They break things. They throw violent tantrums.

But Luca rolls his neck, eyes closed and face calm, then tucks his phone back in his pocket. He plucks a plate off the draining board, lifts his chocolate pop tart from the toaster, and strides from the room without another glance at the camera.

So controlled. Always so controlled.

I mean, I could follow him. Watch him in the other rooms, too.

But I don't. I press June's laptop shut, half-giddy with homesickness.

Luca

Once you've spotted one camera you start seeing them all, watching through the wild thicket of houseplants like panthers' eyes. It's unsettling, not knowing whether Frankie's watching at any given moment or not, but I suppose it's been like this for a while, even if I didn't realize it. She's been watching me. Viewing my life like a soap opera.

She probably knows about my doomed cooking show.

She probably knows *all* my habits, and yet she still watches me. It's liberating.

Has Frankie seen me naked? Has she watched me jerk my cock?

I'm glad, suddenly, that I don't fuck around like most men in my position, because there's no chance Frankie's ever seen me in bed with another girl. Sal's always teased me for it, calling me a monk, but it's a trust thing. I don't let my guard down. Not for anyone, and certainly not for some meaningless fling.

Turns out I never *had* a guard up with Frankie. She sidled

right past it, all before I even knew her name.

At first, I hated the feeling of being watched. When all those alerts went off in my bedroom, I was almost angrier with her than with the hit man, because *I'm* the watcher, damn it. I'm the man who knows everyone's raw little soft spots. No one has shit on me.

But since talking to her a few times… it's different with Frankie.

I don't mind her watching. In fact, as the day wears on, I like it.

I test her, sometimes. It's clear she won't call me just to chat, no matter how much I might want her to. But she'll respond if I prompt her in some way, if it seems like I can't find something or want to ask her about the apartment.

It's funny. She's not even here, and she's the most responsive host you've ever seen.

"Reboot it," she says, calling me mid-morning when I 'accidentally' knock the router off a bookcase. "The password's taped to the bottom."

"Not very secure," I tease her, so glad to hear her husky voice. I set the router back in its place, watching the lights turn green one by one.

Frankie makes a noise like *meh.* The audible version of a shrug. "You can't hack paper."

No, I guess you can't. Though if anyone could, it'd be her.

I last an hour before I need to hear her voice again, then I fill a watering can from the kitchen to the brim and start strolling between rooms, waving it aloft in a visual threat.

"Don't," Frankie blurts as soon as I answer her call. "I watered them two days ago. None of them need it. Seriously, you'll give them root rot."

"Maybe they deserve it. They've been hiding your cameras."

Frankie groans. "Luca! Don't hurt my plants. Please."

I wouldn't. I know by now, even if Frankie hasn't realized yet, that I'd rather wrestle a hundred hit men than make her unhappy, even for a moment.

"Come home, sweetheart," I try next. "I'm getting lonely."

She laughs, and it sounds strangled. High-pitched and breathless. "No way. You're trying to honey trap me. Batting your big, manly eyelashes at the camera. You're acting all flirty and sexy and seductive right now, but when I get there, we both know that's it. It's curtains for Frankie."

Curtains? Who says that?

"I won't hurt you," I promise, then my voice drops. "No more than a nibble."

Frankie's inhale is shaky. "This isn't real," she declares, clearly for her own benefit as much as mine, "and I'm not an idiot, Luca."

I need to leave for a few hours after that. Partly to get some work done, to pick up fresh clothes and check on my apartment, and partly to burn off some of the mounting frustration weighing on my chest. Why won't she come home? Why the fuck did I ever threaten to kill her? Have I ever been more short-sighted in my life?

Talk about a mess.

Frankie won't trust me—and yet every phone call leaves me more addicted.

* * *

One night on Frankie's sofa was bad enough. By the time I'm standing over it at midnight, arms crossed and jaw tight, I'm still not ready for a second.

I don't sleep well. I never have. And stretching out on these hard, lumpy cushions, with my legs bent and my neck craned at a weird angle? It's a lost cause. Maybe I won't even bother.

My phone buzzes in my pocket.

"I do have a bed, you know," Frankie murmurs.

I pinch the bridge of my nose, my whole body crackling to life the way it does when I know she's watching. Suddenly, I feel everything: the warm air on my cheeks; the brush of my cotton shirt against my chest; the coiling tension at the base of my spine. "I was waiting for an invitation."

"Kind of ironic."

I exhale. "Yeah."

When I say I wanted an invitation, I mean I wanted Frankie here, too. Pulling me into her bedroom by the hand, then kicking the door shut behind us and pushing me down onto the messy tangle of her sheets.

Fuck. I'm still not one hundred percent sure what she looks like. I only have that grainy security footage to work with.

"What color are your eyes, sweetheart?" I stroll to her bedroom, my free hand tucked in my pocket.

"Brown," Frankie says slowly. Like she's waiting for the punchline. "Why?"

"I want to picture you. Do you have freckles?"

"Some." There's a pause, and I can practically hear her chewing her lip. "Not many. Do you want me to have freckles?"

It sounds like a line, but I don't care what she looks like. However Frankie is, *that's* how I want her. But how do you say shit like that without sounding like a liar?

"It would give me a game to play," I say instead. "I could join

97

the dots with my tongue." Frankie says nothing, but there's a muted swallow. A distant rustle of fabric. "Where's your friend June tonight?"

"Out on a job."

I frown, coming to a stop at the closed door. "Are you safe while she's gone?"

Frankie's laugh is throaty. "The only person hunting me is you."

"That you know of," I point out, because I'm clearly not the only person she's hacked. Fuck, why does that make me so jealous? Does she watch other men the way she watches me?

"I've never made my presence known before."

I grunt. I'm still pissed off at the thought of her staring at other men through their webcams. It makes my skin hot and itchy under my clothes.

"And I've never... fixated on anyone else." Shit, it's like she can hear my grumpy thoughts. "I grab their info, in and out. So there's way less risk."

I nudge Frankie's bedroom door open, feeling lighter already. "That's good. I don't want you watching others like this."

She makes a loud huff. "Why would I do that?" Wherever the camera is in her bedroom, Frankie must see my sudden grin, because her voice warms like she's in on the joke. "I'm very picky, Luca. Like you and your cooking shows."

"Only the best," I agree, nudging her bedroom door shut then crossing to flick on a bedside lamp. Soft, golden light fills the room, thousands of green leaves casting shadows on the walls. "Can you see me right now?" I flick my top shirt button open. Frankie pauses.

"...Yes."

"And do you like what you see?" I undo another button.

98

Another one. The sides of my shirt sag open as I go, baring my chest to the golden light.

"You know I do," Frankie grits out. "That's why you're doing it. You're playing me."

"No, this isn't a game." I flick open the last button, then shrug one arm out of my shirt. Switch my phone to the other hand, then drop it to the rug in a flutter of white fabric. "Not a bad one, anyway. I mean it. I want you here, sweetheart. I want to taste every inch of you. I want you sighing in my ear."

"But I'm not there," Frankie says, and fuck, I love when she states the obvious. I can picture her adorable little frown; can imagine smoothing it out with my thumb. "And if I were, you'd strangle me sooner than kiss me."

"Not true," I tut, my hand drifting to my belt. "Not true at all. Ah, Frankie, I thought you really knew me by now."

Her silence is heavy. My hacker doesn't like being wrong.

"Have you watched this before, Frankie?" I palm the hard length of my cock through my suit pants. "Have I put on a private show?"

"No." My hacker sounds equal parts irritated and engrossed. "I saw you walk past the kitchen shirtless once, but that's it. I wouldn't have watched you do *that*. Not without you knowing. It would have been creepy, Luca."

True. But surprisingly I don't hate the idea, so long as it was Frankie. I'm strangely disappointed to hear she's kept me so pure.

"Will you watch me now?" My voice is pure gravel. Fuck, I want her. I'm still gripping myself, squeezing and rubbing, but it's not enough like this, muted by the fabric. "I'm going to do it and think of you. Do you want to see that?"

Her silence weighs on me until I think I might suffocate.

"*Frankie.*"

"Yes," she whispers. "I'll watch."

Fuck.

"Touch yourself," I tell her, wrenching at my belt. I want these clothes off right this second. Every part of me is suddenly overheated, too sensitive to every brush of fabric.

"That's not *watching*," Frankie says, but after a moment I hear the catch in her breath. I know she's doing it.

Where is she? In a guest bedroom? Crammed in a corner on an airbed? Sitting at a kitchen table, legs gathered up on her chair?

"Where are you?" I need to know. "Describe the room. Set the scene." My belt slithers free, and then I'm shoving my pants down as she tells me in stilted tones about a sofa, a dark living room, the stars shining through glass balcony doors, and her oversized t-shirt and white cotton panties. Her dark hair gathered in a messy bun.

My boxers go too. I kick everything off then crawl onto Frankie's unmade bed, flopping down onto my back and staring up at the ceiling with the phone pressed to my ear.

The bed covers smell like her. Like soap and black pepper and green leaves, and the very faint scent of sweat. I groan, snatching up a pillow and crushing it to my face. I breathe her in deeply, my hips rocking up against the air.

"You smell so fucking good, sweetheart. I want to rub you all over me."

Frankie chokes out a laugh. "You look insane, Luca."

"I don't care." I toss away the pillow then take my cock in hand, spreading a bead of precum over the head with my thumb. "I know how you smell before I know how you look. *That's* insane."

She hums in agreement, but she can't hide the way her breaths are coming faster. There's more rustling fabric down the phone.

"Are you doing it?" I bark. I sound harsh, but I can't help it. I need fucking details. I've never needed to *know* something so badly in my life. "What are you doing? Are you petting your little clit? Are you fucking yourself on your fingers?"

Frankie moans, the sound ragged. "Yes. *Shit.* Yes, both those things."

"Good." I'm lightheaded, and it must be all the blood in my cock. I've never been so hard. I'm fucking into my own grip, mattress creaking and hips flexing, and I'm rigid in my hand. A steel pipe. "Good girl."

Frankie whimpers, and I grind my teeth. She likes that, huh? Well, there's more where that came from, just as soon as she shows her goddamn face.

I work my cock in a brutal rhythm. Not trying to put on a show like I said, but seeking relief, my nerves sparking under my skin with every little feminine breath in my ear. I fuck my fist like I'm truly alone, like I have no idea she's watching me, like I've thought of so many times since discovering her, and it feels wrong and so fucking right.

The mattress creaks. Sweat beads on my back, then drips onto the sheets. They'll smell like me, now, too. Like the both of us.

"Come home, Frankie." I squeeze myself harder, gripping so tightly it hurts. Jerking myself roughly, like I want to chafe myself raw, punishing myself for scaring her away in the first place. "Say you'll do it. Say you'll come home. Look at this: this cock is yours now. It's waiting for you. Come home and ride it."

Come and drench me in your scent.

Come and claim me like I'm going to claim you.

Frankie lets out a strangled groan. "But you'll hurt me."

"No." I don't want her to even fucking say it. "I will never do that. Because you are *mine*."

Through the phone, I hear her breath seize. I hear her telltale whimpers, and clench my jaw at her helpless squeak. And when Frankie gasps out my name, that's what tips me over the edge; that's what sends hot, white streaks of come lashing over my fist. My body coils up tight, my muscles tensing rock hard, and a tendon stands out in my neck as I groan between my teeth, coming so hard it edges into pain.

Afterward, I stare up at the ceiling, ears ringing. My stomach rises and falls, and I'm burning hot. Covered in a sheen of sweat.

"Frankie," I plead when I can speak again, and I sound broken, even to my own ears. An addict begging for a bigger fix. Maybe that's what softens her in the end.

Because there's a slow exhale. A rustle as she shifts the phone against her ear.

Then: "I'll do it," she says. "I'll come home."

Frankie

I've made a lot of crazy decisions lately, especially where Luca Bianchi is concerned. I consult my dice before I leave June's apartment, scattering them across the scrubbed wood of her kitchen table, but they give me the wrong answer again. They tell me to stay away.

"They're just dice, hon." June wraps an arm around my shoulders, squeezing me into her warmth even though she's smaller than me. I don't know if it's her soft voice or her sunny apartment or her fresh daisy scent, but June always makes me feel like a little kid again, crawling into my mom's lap. "You don't need to listen to them if you don't want to."

Well. I don't regret warning Luca about his hit man, and the dice would have let him die, so... maybe June's right. Maybe I need a new way of making big choices.

I guess I could ask Luca's opinion. That thought nudges at me as I walk the twelve blocks home, my backpack straps cutting into my shoulders. He's smart as hell. And he'd probably give me even better answers than Tabitha, because

Luca knows me more than anyone.

And I know him.

He's not going to hurt me. He's going to keep me, and covet me, and I've known it for a while now. Maybe that's what scared me into staying away.

Because I'm no prize. Some days I can barely look people in the eye, and my houseplants get more vitamins than I do. I have carpal tunnel in my right wrist from spending too many hours on the computer, and I wear baggy clothes so the seams won't bother me.

Luca's going to be so disappointed when he sees me for the first time. Who has he been picturing? Some cute, girly girl like June? An athletic beauty like Tabitha? Instead, he's getting a gremlin in baggy sweatpants.

By the time I reach my building, I'm scowling so hard that the doorman jerks back, palms raised.

"Excuse me," I growl, stomping past to the elevator.

I chose this building because I'm out of place. Because of the faintly horrified expressions of my fancy neighbors whenever I cross the lobby with another grocery bag filled with instant noodles. I *wanted* to be weird, to set people on edge, to shake up their perfect worlds, but as I jab the elevator button, for the first time in my life, I wish I could fit in.

If I wore crisp designer clothes and skillful makeup, I wouldn't look out of place next to the model-handsome Luca Bianchi.

If I could make small talk and tell pleasant jokes with strangers, maybe he could take me on dates. Introduce me to people as his girlfriend.

But I don't do those things. I'm not that girl, and as the elevator swoops upward, my black mood gathers around me like storm clouds. I bet he's not even there. I bet he got what he wanted—my agreement to come home—then promptly lost interest. I bet he over-watered my plants, too.

I bet, I bet.

Grump, grump, grump.

I stomp so hard down the hallway to my apartment that the door swings open before I reach it.

"Hello." Luca leans in the doorway, arms crossed over his toned chest, his mossy eyes sparkling with amusement. "What put you in such a snit? I heard you coming from three blocks away."

"No, you didn't," I say pointlessly. Obviously he didn't. Luca knows how to make jokes, because he is a normal human being. The jerk.

Sighing, Luca pushes my door wider, then steps back to let me inside. Immediately, I'm hit with the muggy, green scent of my apartment, and some of my anger settles. Checking the first few pots, I find dry soil. Not parched, but not soggy.

"I didn't water them." Luca stands at my back, arms still crossed, and his voice is harder now. He's defensive. "You can check every single pot, or you can take my word for it."

Somehow I think there's a right answer here.

"I know you didn't." My elevator tantrum aside, it wouldn't have been elegant. Luca doesn't make sloppy plays. "But houseplants are tricky. Sometimes they get thirsty and sometimes they don't."

"I see." Luca waits while I kick off my sneakers and drop my backpack to the floor, then make my way down the hall. I check every pot, even the ones where I need to climb onto a chair or table top. Luca sighs when I do that, moving close enough to catch me if I fall.

Should I have greeted him before the plants? How can I do that when he's so handsome I can barely look straight at him?

"Which one is your favorite?" I ask part way round the living room, spinning a peace lily to give the rear leaves more light.

Luca thinks for a moment, then mutters, "The one on the bookcase with the vines."

"English Ivy."

He exhales again. "Yeah. I guess so." Luca really sighs a lot around me. He's lucky he's in a room with so many plants, or he might become oxygen deprived.

He's mad at me. This first meeting isn't what he wanted. Because *I'm* not what he wanted? Sometimes I hate being right. Should have listened to those dice.

"Well?" The mobster waits until I've checked every last plant in my apartment. We're standing in my bedroom, staring at each other across the expanse of my bed. The covers are straightened, the pillows fluffed and piled up. It's the first time the bed's been made since I bought it.

"Well what?" I'm not good with open questions, and last night Luca lay there naked and touched himself. A very distracting memory. I saw it all on June's laptop screen, and my abdomen feels heavier just thinking about it, aching and warm.

Luca huffs and spreads his arms. He's wearing a dove gray shirt and black pants today, and the fabric shifts against his toned chest when he moves, tension pulling on the buttons.

I frown at them, mentally urging one to pop open.

"Do you want me to leave, Frankie?"

I dart a glance at Luca's face. His jaw is hard, his eyes narrowed. He was so happy to see me only a few minutes ago.

"If you want," I mumble. I'm sure not going to beg him to stay. A girl's gotta have some dignity, and I've been running short lately.

"So that's it." Luca props one hand on his hip, rubbing the other over his jaw. Watching me with those cold, assessing eyes. "You hack me, you phone-fuck me, and now you're done. Am I not what you wanted? You've watched me enough. You knew what you were signing up for."

I shrug, so miserable. I knew he'd have second thoughts, but I didn't think I'd screw it up *this* quickly. This conversation barreled off the rails the second I stepped through the door, and I have no idea how to force it back on track.

"You're either very brave or very stupid, Frankie." I choke out a laugh. I'm neither of those things, but there's a real warning in Luca's eyes. They're dark and glittering. "But once I walk out that door, you can't watch me anymore. Do you understand? I can't allow it. Next time I won't be so forgiving."

Threats, always threats. I wet my lips. "I won't watch you."

Luca's expression hardens even more. "Well, then," he says, and then he's striding around the bed. Yanking me close by the elbow, and kissing me hard enough to bruise. I make the world's most embarrassing squawking noise, and it's my first kiss, so there's no way I'm any good. But Luca lets me wind my arms around his neck, burying my fingers in his bronze hair, and he growls with approval when I crush myself against his chest.

"I liked you better on the phone," he snarls, and yeah. That's it. That's the moment when I crack open down the middle. Luca Bianchi might as well have buried an ax in my rib cage.

"I'm not good with people." I press the words against his neck, voice shaking.

A harsh laugh. "No shit."

It's my first kiss, and that's supposed to be happy, I think. Romantic, even. But though Luca makes my nerves spark to life, though he overwhelms my senses in the best way, I'm too raw and hollow to really enjoy it.

He nips my bottom lip. I pull away.

Luca Bianchi steps back, face carefully blank. A stranger to me again.

He reaches out, ruffling my dark bangs with a fingertip. "Be seeing you, Frankie. Stay out of my fucking tech."

Then he turns around... and he's gone.

* * *

With time to replay our meeting over and over in my head, I can see all the points where I went wrong. Luca was excited to see me; I was so nervous I ignored him for the houseplants. He wanted smiles; I scowled at him. He asked if I didn't want him, and all I did was shrug and say he could leave.

This is why I'm better online. In written form. I can have time to think, to read the situation, to figure out what I really want to say.

When I crawl into bed after a long, scalding shower, my sheets smell like him. It's still morning, but I don't care. I'm gonna sleep all day. I recognize Luca's scent from our kiss, but I like to think I'd know it either way. It's so him. Storm clouds and smoky cologne. Sharp and electric and unforgiving.

I bury my face in the pillows and sigh. I don't cry—much. What is there to cry over? I was always going to screw it up.

But as I bury my face in soft cotton that smells like him, I sure wish Luca Bianchi would let me watch him for a while

Frankie

longer.

Luca

This is a very bad time for my cousin Sal to try to kill me. Hours after leaving my hacker, I need to *think*, damn it, to go over where I went wrong with Frankie. My instincts are screaming at me, squirming in my brain, letting me know that I missed something big.

I hate missing things. It feels like fucking amateur hour, and I didn't live to my thirties in *this* family by stepping wrong. I know people. I play them like fiddles.

All except Frankie.

I've never felt out of control like that. Exposed and raw, like a nerve. Hurt and embarrassed and so pissed off. I was cruel with her, harsher than I needed to be, and though she rejected me first, it's not sitting right in my stomach.

I liked you better on the phone.

Why the hell did I say that? When I close my eyes, I can feel the exact way she stiffened against me. The way she went wooden in my arms, practically vibrating with hurt.

I meant that she seemed to like *me* better on the phone,

and I preferred that dynamic. I liked her breathy and eager and sweet in my ear, not stomping around and ignoring me, huffing like she couldn't wait for me to leave.

Maybe I read it all wrong. Maybe I made a fool of myself.

Thinking about the way I touched myself for her... I screw my eyes shut, my face hot.

"Luca," the boss clips out. "Are we keeping you awake?"

We're gathered in his study, surrounded by polished dark wood and bookcases groaning with leather hardbacks that have never been cracked. All his inner circle are here, getting an update on business. Movements in our territory. Plans for the politicians. I should be listening, because this is my area. I'm the one who pulls all the strings.

"No, sir." I force myself to listen, ignoring the excited way Sal's preening across the room. Yeah, he definitely thinks he's in line for my job. Bullshit. I meet his eyes, expression hard, and the asshole nearly wets his pants.

I need to deal with my cousin. Sal's a loose end, and I've got bigger problems.

But bigger problems or no, another hit man broke into my apartment when I was gone. Ola told me about the damage he left, the broken door and boot prints, whispering in my ear when I came home to change. Her hands were white-knuckled on her mop handle.

I sent her home and told her to stay away until it's safe. I'll pay her either way, but I don't need Ola's death on my conscience. Plus I love those perogies.

"Luca," the boss says, "go round the members' clubs today. I want dirt on the new candidates. And take one of these assholes with you."

"Sal," I say, eyes fixed on my cousin as my smile spreads wide.

111

He goes chalk white, wriggling in his chair. "I'll take Sal."

"Good." A meaty hand waves in the air, dismissing us. We all stand, wood chairs creaking in relief. "Get it done."

Oh, I will.

* * *

I call Frankie in the early evening from a pig farm twenty miles outside the city, watching hundreds of muddy swine chew up the body of my cousin. It gives me no pleasure except the satisfaction of a task ticked off my list, and the knowledge that the hit men should stop coming for me—for a while, at least.

The boss won't be happy about this. But he's never happy, so what's new?

And he won't care once he hears about the hit men. At the risk of sounding like a child on the schoolyard, Sal started it.

Pigs are good for this. See, who needs a cleaner anyway? These pigs are doing a better job of body disposal than Sal ever did, eating him bones, boots and all, and standing out in the countryside is almost restful if you can get past the crunching.

Frankie takes a long time to pick up. For a minute, I worry she's tossed her latest burner away already—or worse, that I fucked up so badly that she'll never speak to me again.

"Hello?" Her voice is wobbly and thin.

"Frankie." Surely no one else would call this number, but she still sucks in a shocked breath when she hears my voice.

"Oh. Luca."

Yeah.

Oh, Luca is about all I deserve after some of the stuff I said to her. The more distance I get from this morning, the more our meeting changes in my mind. It's like I'm viewing it from new angles. From her cameras, maybe, tucked away between the leaves.

I don't look good in these reruns.

Because Frankie was tense. Terrified. So nervous it infected me too, set me on edge, and what did I do? Did I set her at ease? No. I escalated.

I threatened to kill her all those days ago, and then when I finally lured her home, I lost my temper with her. Fuck, *I* ought to be in there with those pigs.

"Um," she says, because I haven't spoken yet. Too busy kicking my own ass. "What's up?"

"Nothing much." I squint into the sunset, at the dying rays of bloody light. "Getting rid of a body. You remember Salvatore?"

There's a long pause. Then, so hollow: "Are you threatening me again? I said I won't watch you anymore."

Thud. That's the feeling of my heart slamming to the base of my rib cage, dropping a sickening way down my body. I've really fucked up if Frankie's still scared of me. And I dig the heel of my palm into my eye, grinding hard enough to hurt as I stare out over the rolling grassy hills.

"I'm not threatening you, sweetheart."

Another soft noise. "Sweetheart, huh? You really do like me better on the phone."

Ah, shit. "I shouldn't have said that to you. I didn't mean it like that."

"Yes, you did."

"I *didn't*. I loved you in person too. Are you kidding me? With those cute little bangs? Those retro sneakers? I just didn't love you pushing me away like that." I swallow hard, pulse thudding in my ears, but she's still not saying anything. I keep going. "You were so beautiful and clever and you wouldn't even look at me, Frankie. After everything we did. Do you know how badly I wanted you to look at me?"

"I was nervous," she whispers. I squeeze the phone until it creaks. "I didn't mean to be rude. I just—I panicked."

Fuck. My heart. "I know. I know that now. Please let me come back. We'll try again, okay? And you'll look at me, and I won't be an asshole."

"What if I don't?" Frankie wails, so loud I hold the phone away from my ear. "What if I can't?" And she sounds so melodramatic that I have to laugh. It bursts out of me, echoing over the hillside. The closest pigs pause their chewing, snorting at me before they duck back down for another bite.

It's no way to go, chewed up on a pig farm. But then, Sal doesn't care anymore, does he?

"Stop laughing!" She's telling me off, but I can hear the reluctant smile in her voice. We're getting somewhere, thank god. The ice is thawing. "That was my first kiss, and look how it ended! I don't know if I can do *any* of this, Luca."

That sobers me up. "I didn't know it was your first."

"Would you have been sweeter?"

My mouth twists. "Probably not." I am who I am. "I was so fucking hungry for you, I could barely see straight. But I wouldn't have left like that. And there would have been second and third kisses, Frankie. Other things, too."

She blows out a slow breath. "...Yeah? What other things?"

She's giving me an opening. I gaze up at the heavens. Thank god.

"What else would I have done to you?" I wait for the last scrap of Sal disappear, then turn on my heel and stride away in my rubber boots. The farmer knows better than to come out and talk to me while I'm here, so it's a clear walk back to the mud-splattered car. I put her on speaker as I fold into the driver's seat. "I can tell you, Frankie, but I'd rather show you in person. I'll need a shower first, though. I smell like pig farm."

She giggles, and it's the sweetest sound filling the car. I flex my grip on the steering wheel, pulling over the bumpy track toward the highway. The evening light is soft, tinted the exact same shade of pink as her lips.

"You can shower here," Frankie offers, so shy.

I tilt the rear view mirror, watching Sal's final resting place slide into the distance. "I'm on my way."

Frankie

He's coming back. Oh my god, Luca's coming back. I stand at the foot of my bed, body frozen and mind racing at a hundred miles per hour. Should I bathe? No, I already did that. Should I clean? Well, he's already seen my mess.

Oh, god. What if I can't look at him again? What if I screw it up for good this time?

Because Luca Bianchi should come with a warning. I knew he was beautiful, obviously, but seeing him through a webcam or in photos online versus seeing him in person were very different experiences. It was like spotting a mountain lion a few feet away instead of in a grainy photo on a news website, staring at you from the roadside and looking hungry.

My heart rate spiked. Adrenaline coursed through my body.

And I turned into a complete idiot.

If I had more warning this time, a few days to prepare, I'd make extra sure that Luca feels welcome when he gets here. Maybe I'd buy him some kitchen equipment, or fresh ingredients for the fridge. Maybe I'd set out a towel for him, like this is a hotel, and put a foil-wrapped chocolate on his pillow.

Hey, I've got towels. I can do that right now.

I pick out my favorite one for him, a fluffy midnight blue one, and brush off any tiny specks of lint before balancing it on the bathroom counter top.

"Um." My voice bounces off the tiles. I've never invited a man here before. I never *really* invited Luca the first time—he just showed up. Will he expect something? A freshly made drink pushed into his hand? A peck on the cheek like a 1950s housewife?

Sinking slowly into my panic, I stare at the white bathroom tiles and forget to blink. My brain's buzzing and rattling around in my skull, and I should *do* something. Change out of my sweatpants and baggy black t-shirt, maybe. Wash up the bowl and mug from my lunch.

God knows how long I stand there staring. However long it takes to drive here from a pig farm, I guess, because a brisk knock on my door makes me jump.

"Shit." I slip out of the bathroom and tiptoe down the hall. Like if he doesn't hear me coming, that evens things up somehow. "Double shit."

Luca stares at me when I pull the door open. Too late, I remember I went to bed with wet hair and now my head looks like a bird's nest.

My gaze skates away from his mossy green eyes. Travels down his toned chest and gray button-down shirt; his black suit pants and leather shoes. He must have worn those farmer boots out in the country, because there are splatters of mud on his pants, but they start just below the knee.

I wrinkle my nose and address his stomach. "You really do smell bad."

Luca huffs a laugh. He tips my chin up, waiting until I meet his eyes again, and the smile that spreads over his face…

It's warm. So delicious, like sinking into a hot bath. It's impossible not to smile back.

"Hello, Frankie."

I force my lungs to work again. Wrap my hand around his wrist. "Hi, Luca." With a tug, I pull him inside before he can change his mind.

* * *

"This is your towel." I point needlessly at the blue heap on the bathroom counter.

Luca nods at it solemnly. "Nice to meet you." He's very silly for a mobster. I didn't realize that from watching through his webcam.

I brush past him to get the water going, but keep one eye fixed on the large mirror above the sink. Luca's undressing. He knows I'm watching, too, because he winks at me, flicking his shirt buttons open one by one.

I get this swooping sense of deja vu, and then I'm gone again. My brain has fritzed out, and all I can do is stand there like an idiot and watch him out of the corner of my eye.

"You're welcome to join me." Luca tugs his belt through the loops, the tendons in his forearms flexing. "Do you have another towel?"

Wordlessly, I leave the room to fetch one. By the time I come back, I'm breathing normally again.

I wouldn't say it's going well, not exactly. I'm clearly acting like a crazy person, but Luca doesn't seem mad this time. He seems accepting. Even fond. And when I step back into the bathroom, nudging palm fronds aside so I can close the door behind me, Luca smiles at me in warm, shirtless welcome.

"I wasn't sure you'd come back." He takes my pink towel, still damp from this morning, and places it beside his on the counter.

I frown at the shower spray. Steam curls toward the ceiling. "Where else would I go?"

Luca hums. "Nowhere, I hope." Then his hands are on me, warm and dry and so much bigger than mine.

He squeezes my shoulders. Kneads the small muscles until my tension drains away, gazing at me softly the whole time. And once my shoulders slump and I sway in his hold, he starts touching me in other places, too.

He runs his hands down my arms, the tiny hairs standing on end like I've been electrified. He rubs circles onto my palms with his thumbs, and then he reaches up again. Cups my neck; strokes my jaw; ruffles my bangs.

"You like doing that."

His teeth flash as he grins. "So I do."

I don't mind. My mom used to say that if there was anything in my favor, it's that I'm not vain. Luca can do anything he likes to my hair.

Since he's touching me so much, I figure I'm allowed to touch him back. I start simple, resting my palms on the hard swells of muscle of his chest. Brown hair dusts his bare skin, and lower down, his stomach is ridged. I can feel his heartbeat thumping beneath my hand.

"Will you kiss me again?"

Luca leans down, his nose brushing mine before our lips

meet. It's gentler than earlier. Hazier, too. Like we're sinking into each other, tongues moving in a slow, lazy dance.

Heat coils around us. The air gets thick and muggy. When we break away, my chest feels like it's bursting with tiny bubbles.

"You really do stink, Luca."

His laugh echoes over the drumming spray.

He gets in first, kicking the rest of his clothes off and stepping behind the glass pane. I watch him hungrily, pleased that it's *my* bar of soap he's running over his body. My shampoo he's working into his hair. After this, Luca won't smell like pig farm. He'll smell like me. His hair looks darker when it's wet, fully brown instead of bronze, and rivulets of hot water streak his bare skin.

I tug my baggy t-shirt off, letting it drop to the tiles beside his things. I make sure the fabric is touching.

"You're not wearing a bra." Luca's words rasp through the steamy air. Green eyes watch me, narrowed and intent.

"I don't like seams and straps. Don't like stuff close to my skin."

"Good." Is it? "Pinch your nipples."

Ha. He's so bossy, even when he's in there and I'm out here. I do what he says, though, plucking and pinching my nipples and watching him stare at me through the foggy glass, and it feels even better doing this with his eyes on me. Everything's more sensitive. Amplified. Like there's a direct line between my nipples and my pussy, and every pinch makes me ache harder down there. Makes me swollen, slick and needy.

I already know what Luca's cock looks like. I saw it through the camera last night and I can see it now, stiff and ruddy, jutting out into the air. It bobs when he moves, and when he soaps it up, he gives it an extra squeeze, letting out a hiss.

"I want to come in now."

Luca booms another laugh, taking his hands away. "Were you waiting for an invitation? Yes, Frankie. Please come and join me."

* * *

My sweatpants and underwear drop in a rustle of fabric, then I step under the hot spray. The steam's thicker in here, and it smells like soap. No more pig farm, only clean, wet Luca Bianchi. He makes space for me, backing up respectfully against the shower wall, though his eyes are still hungry. A mountain lion watching a jogger.

"You're not in the water anymore."

A muscled shoulder lifts. "I'm letting you wash."

"But you'll get cold."

Luca grins, then joins me under the spray. He was right—I get a lot less water now, and this isn't very efficient, but I bathed this morning. I'm not here to get clean, I'm here to touch Luca's skin when it's slippery and flushed.

And he feels *good.* Hard and wet and wonderful, his big hands roaming over my bare body as his pulse beats under his skin.

The broad head of his cock brushes at my stomach. Too curious to think twice, I reach down and tuck it between my legs, squeezing his hard shaft between my thighs. I like how it feels down there. Like sitting on a sexy broomstick, slotting thick and perfect between my lips and grazing against my clit.

"Oh, *fuck.*" Luca grips my hips, sawing his cock back and forth between my legs. His forehead presses against mine, and our stomachs brush together with every thrust. "Shit, Frankie. I didn't expect that."

I tell him my broomstick comparison. He shakes his head, expression strained as he stares at the wall. "There's no way I'm coming out of this with any dignity."

I can't imagine Luca Bianchi ever *not* being dignified, no matter what ridiculous thing I say to him. He's so sharp and clever and elegant. So primal and deadly. But he clearly needs some reassurance, so I trail open-mouthed kisses up his throat, tugging on a handful of his wet hair.

When I look up at him again, Luca must feel better already, because he crowds me against the shower wall, caging me in with his hands pressed on the tiles either side of my head.

"Do I still stink, Frankie?"

I shake my head dumbly. "No."

"And do you want me right now? Do you want my cock?"

A nod this time. "Yes." Hell, if the questions are all this easy, I'll nail this quiz. I trail my palms over Luca's stomach to celebrate. "You have a nice body, Luca. The best."

His throat bobs. "So do you."

And it's not enough. I've told him I like his body, and that's true, but it's so low on the list of my favorite things about him. I like his deep voice and his three phones and his friendship with his cleaner Ola. I like that he makes pasta from scratch, and I like that his green eyes are the color of houseplant foliage. I liked watching him eat my popcorn, and I like that he called me from the pig farm. I like that he came back for me again, even when I pushed him away so badly the first time.

"I love everything about you, Luca."

My words are so hoarse, I'm surprised he hears them, but he must because he groans and flattens me against the tiles. He's rocking against me again, sliding his cock against my stomach, but I don't feel used. I feel so, so wanted.

"So do I, sweet girl." He latches onto my neck, sucking hard, and I scrabble at his shoulders for purchase. "I didn't understand before, but I do now. Okay? You're perfect, Frankie. My perfect girl."

He leans back long enough to spin me around, then pushes me against the tiles.

"Brace yourself." His right hand strokes along my arm, then tangles our fingers together. "It's going to feel strange at first, but we'll go slow. If it hurts, you say so and we'll stop. Alright?"

I nod, water from my wet hair trickling into my eyes. I blink it away, then I'm screwing my eyes shut for a different reason, because Luca's *there.* Pushing inside me, his free hand steadying my hip.

"Okay?" His lips brush against my shoulder. "Sweetheart. Answer me."

"I'm okay," I wheeze. "It's… it's a lot."

"Yeah." Luca stops pushing for a second, reaching around to play with my nipples. Every brush and pinch of his fingers makes me soften up down there. Makes me warm and slick and pliant, sucking his cock deeper into my body.

"Keep going," I say when I can't stand it anymore. "Go further in."

Another kiss against my neck, and then he's sliding deeper. The stretch burns a little, but it's not painful exactly. It's just so *much.*

"Stop," I gasp after a few more inches. Luca stops at once, his heart thumping against my back. "Just for a second," I add, and I can feel him relax. "You're really big."

"Ah, yes." Luca tweaks my nipple again. "There's my ego.

Hello, old friend."

"Shut up."

His chuckle vibrates through my whole body, and *god*, that feels good. I reach back and slap at his hip. "Okay, more. More. And laugh again."

"I can't laugh on command, Frankie," Luca says, though he's chuckling as he says it. Chuckling and thrusting harder against me, his hips snapping against my ass. He fucks deeper and deeper, forcing his way inside me, and it feels so good that I stumble against the tiles.

"Careful." Luca hitches me upright then flattens me against the wall. Pins me there with his bulk, his cock plunging between my legs.

The air is thick with steam. It's hot in here, the shower spray pounding against the floor.

"Do you like this?" He licks my throat. Scrapes my pulse point with my teeth. And green eyes watch me closely over my shoulder, even as his length stretches and fills my pussy. "Frankie. Do you like this?"

"Yes." It comes out as a groan. Do I *like* this? I want to do this every day, every hour, every *minute* for the rest of our lives, and I tell him so, my confession muted by the drumming spray.

"Every minute could be a challenge." Luca's squeezing me so tight, like he doesn't want to let go of me either. "We'll work on the rest." And then, like he hasn't been holding back a devious secret weapon, Luca reaches down my body and starts rubbing my clit.

"Jesus!" I buck back against him, then thrust forward against his hand. I don't know what to chase more, his cock or his fingers. Whichever one I go after, I miss the other, and they're

124

working in concert. Heightening every brush of contact until I'm tense and shuddering, sparks coursing under my skin. I'm burning up, smoldering, gasping for breath, and for once my thoughts aren't swirling around my head. I'm nothing but a body. A pulsing, needy body.

Luca's teeth scrape my shoulder, and he rubs my clit faster. "I didn't get to see you come last night, Frankie. Show me now."

I whimper. Try to surrender to tension building in my belly, the heat and ache and crackle of delicious friction, and once I let it drag me under, there's no going back. I screw my eyes shut as it washes over me, sweeps me up like a violent storm, then I collapse against the shower wall as I shudder and quake.

My fingers dig into the shower tiles, their tips turning white, and I clamp down so hard on Luca's cock that he feels *huge,* impossibly bigger.

"Fuck." His thrusts are jerkier now, rough and uneven. He presses me hard against the tiles, grips the back of my neck, and empties inside me with a groan.

Hot water speckles my cheeks and drips in my eyes. A different wet heat spreads between my legs.

We come back into our bodies slowly, breathing hard. Luca pulls out gingerly, and sticky fluid trickles down my thighs. We rinse off under the shower spray with gentle touches.

"Beautiful girl." He can't stop stroking me, kissing me, playing with my hair. "Perfect girl."

If he says so.

I get out first, passing Luca the blue towel. He watches me the whole time he dries off, then kicks his stinky pig farm clothes into the corner with a wrinkled nose. "Guess I'll stay naked."

125

I can't hide my grin. Because Luca Bianchi is *here*. He's really here.

He's staying. He's naked.

And he's mine.

Luca

F
   our years later

   I feel her eyes on me the minute I step through the
   door. Dark camera lenses watch me from between
thousands of waxy green leaves, but I don't react as I shrug off
my jacket. I hang it on the coat hook, then kick my shoes off
and roll my neck with a sigh.

I'm a little messier since moving in with Frankie. More laid
back.

It's not a bad thing.

You know what else is great for learning to relax? Faking
your own death. Fuck, I've never felt so free. Frankie helped
me do it, and she still keeps tabs on my old family, even
years later. She watches for anyone who might come sniffing
around, wondering about me, but in all this time, no one's
even questioned what happened.

As far as they're concerned, I disappeared with Sal. Someone
must have picked us off when we were outside the territory.

A shame, but it's the cost of business.

We had to leave the city, obviously. Couldn't risk being recognized. So we moved hundreds of miles away and started over, hiring a massive van for all her damn houseplants. But it felt good, it felt *right*, and I left enough money behind for Ola to retire. And one good thing about the plants is that we felt right at home here straight away.

Our home is an indoor jungle of giant leaves and trailing vines. It smells like damp soil and green matter, and as I stroll down the hallway, I half expect to hear the shriek of monkeys or the cawing of birds. Instead, all I hear is the distant rattle of a keyboard.

My wife is home, then. Watching me—and everyone else in this city. That's good. The two of us, we work together these days, dealing in peoples' dirty secrets. Business is booming. There are so many. An inexhaustible supply.

I reach the baby's room, poking my head inside. The crib's opposite the window, the late afternoon sun drifting hazily through the glass. There are plants in here too, though Frankie picked out special ones with bright yellow flowers.

I check on our daughter. Smooth her blanket and stroke her cheek. She stirs, so I back off, tugging my collar open.

Every time I look at my daughter or my wife, my heart swells so much that my chest could explode. I won't wake her, though. Not while I've got a shot at some time with Frankie, and I pull the door closed as I leave.

There are cameras in there too, obviously. We'll know if she needs us.

"What's for dinner?" Frankie asks the second I step into her office. I grin, brushing a trailing spider plant off my shoulder as I cross to her side. Her monitors loom all around her, one showing the baby's room, another showing the hallway I just walked down. The rest are bank statements; someone's email inbox; lines of code.

"Didn't you miss me?"

She's curled up on her desk chair, feet tucked under her ass. She gets pins and needles sitting like that, but she still does it. Frankie hums as I brush her hair away from her neck, nibbling at her earlobe.

"Of course. I always miss you." She swats at me, and I straighten with a laugh. Her fingers fly over the keyboard, so fast they nearly blur. "And I miss your cooking, too."

"Then I'll make you a deal." Her stiff shoulders relax as I knead them, and she melts back against her chair, still typing. "Stop working for a second and let me eat what *I* want, and I'll cook whatever you ask for tonight."

Frankie's silent for a long time. She's weighing the pros and cons. On the one hand, she doesn't like stopping her work in the middle. Frankie is a focus machine. On the other hand... well, it's a no-brainer, isn't it? She gets her pussy eaten and the food of her choice. After a while I get bored of deliberations, spinning her around in her chair.

"Hey!" She sounds outraged, but she's smiling. Already wriggling her legs out from under her, pulling her baggy t-shirt over her head. She throws it at me and I catch it, the fabric warm from her skin. "You're so bossy, Luca."

I grin, bending to work her waistband over her hips. "Yes, this must be terrible for you." Her mischievous smile lights up my insides.

"I want pizza tonight."

"Alright."

"And I want to watch you spin it in the air."

She drives a hard bargain. I kneel between her bare legs. "Agreed."

Frankie cards her fingers through my hair, and I push her thighs wide. I've only been gone for a few hours, but that's far too long to be away from her.

"Did you learn any good secrets today, sweetheart?"

Frankie smirks. "Always."

I duck down to breathe against her pussy. "Tell me everything."

III

Honey Trap

Description

He's the one man who knows better than to trust me...

And I want him so badly it hurts.

People say I have a friendly face. That I'm a good listener. All I know is ever since I was a little girl, people have told me their secrets–even the terrible ones.

The good news? Those dirty secrets fetch a high price.

The bad news? The gorgeous P.I knows how I make a living, and he'll barely say a word to me.

Oh, he'll sit near me and nod hello. He'll look out for me and keep me safe. He's oddly protective for a man who doesn't trust me an inch.

But he doesn't need to worry. I'd never spill *his* secrets, and whenever he's near…

For once, I'm the one saying too much.

June

The bar stool beside me is empty, but it's only a matter of time. The room is crowded and loud, the air muggy from so many bodies, and I won't be solo for more than a few minutes. My mama used to say I have a *quality*. Something about me invites people closer—especially men—and I never sit alone for long before a stranger plonks down beside me and strikes up a conversation.

It used to bother me. I never asked them over, you know? And sometimes a girl wants to be left alone to do the puzzle in the paper. Besides, I don't trust a man who flirts with a stranger. For all he knows, I'm crazier than a bag of cats. It's not smart.

But after a few years of politely sending people away I discovered the benefit, because for some reason, people tell me all kinds of wild things. I'm a walking, talking confession booth, and folks line up around the block to tell me all their dirty secrets.

Secrets are useful, especially in this city.

Secrets can fetch a high price.

And secrets keep my grandma comfy and safe in her special nursing home. So you think I mind being interrupted these days? Hell no. I practically kick the stool out, begging for someone to sit down.

I'm after something juicy tonight. The last few weeks, I've had a string of unhappy wives hire me, asking me to attend certain bars then report back whether their husbands flirt with me or not. I take those jobs, because grandma's bills seem to get fatter every month, but I don't feel good about them. They always leave a sour taste in my mouth.

They put me off men, too, that's for sure. There's no honor left around here.

"Another drink, June-bug?"

The ancient bartender, Harry, braces his hands against the wood and smiles at me, face creasing into a thousand wrinkles. Thin black braces cut two stripes over his rounded shoulders, his pinstriped shirt baggy beneath. Harry knows I'm working, and he leaves me be except for bringing me drinks. He's a sweetheart. I have a sneaking suspicion he used to take my grandma on dates.

My throat *is* dry. I flick a longing glance at the brown bottles of ginger ale in the fridge, but I'd better not. If I keep an empty glass in front of me, that's another temptation for a stranger to sit down.

And I'm not after just anyone's secrets tonight. A politician's coming in here. My hacker friend Frankie tipped me off, and everyone knows this guy is crooked as hell. With his dodgy business ties and his wandering hands in the office, he's a scandal waiting to happen.

And me? Well, I'd be delighted to help that process along.

"No thanks, Harry." The bartender raps the bar with his knuckles and moves away, and I catch a flash of movement in the hazy mirror over his shoulder. The whole bar stretches out in the glass, the sizes and distances all warped, and this is how I keep watch on who's coming and going behind my back.

Two things draw my eye right now: number one, the politician and two lackeys pushing through the doorway, shrugging off their dark coats, their smiles sharp. So confident that they're the predators in this jungle. And number two: a certain dark-haired private investigator scowling at me from a nearby booth.

Marcus Miller. We move in the same circles, live in the same shades of gray, but he always looks so pissed off to find me working. Like he wants to send me home to bed without any dinner. He's gripping a beer bottle tight, practically strangling the neck, and his piercing blue eyes are pinned to the back of my head.

Maybe he's here for the politician, too. It happens some-times—we end up jockeying for the same clients, digging for the same information. Of course, Marcus doesn't rely on his pretty face, not with that scowl and the pale scar slashed down one cheek, so he uses other methods. He's stealthier. More intimidating, too.

Maybe that's why he disapproves of me so much.

It's kind of a pity, because a single glimpse of Marcus Miller makes my tummy flutter.

With effort, I drag my gaze back to the politician in the mirror. He's scanning the bar, looking for a good booth or a pair of pretty legs, his thinning blond hair all puffed up from the wind. He's shameless about it, in the way over-confident men always are. He feels like he's owed this. That the world should lay down in front of him and let him step on all its squishy bits.

Chewing my lip, I swivel on my stool by an inch. Give the politician a glimpse of bare, tanned thigh below the hem of my dress, all while stabbing at the melting ice in my glass with a straw. Highlighting my empty drink.

Come on. Come on. Come over here.

I'm a saucer of milk left out for a tom cat. A ripe, juicy blackberry in the hedgerow.

The second he sees me, the politician's smile gets even sharper. I watch it all in the mirror from beneath my lowered lashes: the stark hunger that plays over his face; the way he nudges one of his lackeys and nods at me; the way he strolls over to greet me alone, his hands shoved in his pockets.

"You look thirsty." I jump like I'm surprised, wheeling around to blink up at him. I don't have to crane my neck too far. This guy's shorter than he looks on TV—probably only a few inches taller than me. I bet he wears those stacked heels.

"Oh!" My hand flutters near my chest, not quite landing. His gaze tracks the movement, and he shuffles closer another inch, like he'll touch the front of my dress on my behalf. I pretend to gather myself, recovering from the shock and overwhelming pleasure of being greeted by a man like *him.* "I watched you on my television this morning!"

The politician grabs the free stool. He sits on it, gesturing for Harry. "Did you? And did you like what you saw?"

No.

I beam at him, warm and friendly. "I sure did. You sounded ever so smart."

His teeth are extra white when he grins. "That's because I am, sweetheart."

The politician orders a whiskey from Harry, and a vodka cranberry for me. He doesn't even ask what I'd like, just assumes that he knows me with one glance. I smile and giggle and thank him, obviously, but when I risk another glance at the P.I in the mirror, Marcus rolls his eyes.

I press my lips together, fighting a *true* smile.

Marcus knows I hate vodka. On the rare occasions he'll deign to sit with me, he always orders my favorite ginger ale, and he never tells me a single secret. He knows better than that, but lord, I wish he would.

I'd never spill Marcus's secrets. Never.

And he'd never do anything slimy like this guy, anyway.

It's impossible not to compare the two men who are focused on me right now. The politician has zoomed right past faux-charming to dismissive, like he's already judging me for sleeping with him before I've even done it. I'm not going to, obviously, but *he* doesn't know that. Asshole.

Marcus, meanwhile, has his customary scowl, but it's not like he's judging me. He's protective.

Though both men look to be in their mid-thirties, Marcus takes way better care of himself, too. His skin has a healthier glow; his black hair is thick and his shoulders are broad with muscle. For a brief, dizzying moment, I want him beside me so badly my head spins.

"It's going to be huge." The politician's bragging about some project that he's spearheading. A renovation of the city docks. "It'll change the whole face of the city. And you know, there are millions of dollars involved. *Millions.*"

I bet. The docks are mob territory, and there's no way

they're not greasing his palms. Keeping some areas untouched; working others to their specific requirements. I trace my fingertip over the rim of my glass, gazing at him like he's my hero.

"Oh, wow. Tell me *everything*."

He does, too. Or more than he should, anyway, and when he stands to use the bathroom forty minutes later, he's got that unsettled look on his face. The one that comes from accidentally blurting out more than you planned; from suddenly realizing you're not as in control as you thought.

I see that look a lot.

"We're leaving when I get back," he clips at me, like this will reassert his dominance. I'd bet my last dollar that his one night stands have the worst time. "Fetch your coat now. Don't keep me waiting."

I nod, sweet and eager. And the second he disappears into the bathroom, I hop down from my stool just like he said.

I don't fetch my coat, though. I squeeze behind the bar, winking at Harry, and go to hide out in the back room until the politician's gone. I keep a stack of old newspapers back there, and I'm working through the crosswords every chance I get.

He thinks I'm so dumb because I've got a pretty face and a pair of boobs. But I'm not the one who just confessed to corruption in a crowded bar, am I?

Marcus

It's always unsettling watching June work. It's almost
supernatural, the way she draws people closer, the way
she tricks information out of men. God knows if I'd met
her like this, bumbling past in a bar, I might've sat down beside
her too, though it's not my usual style.

I might have bought her a drink. Tried to ask her on a
date, and asked all about her life, and told her anything she
wanted to know. Fool that I am, after an hour of her smiles,
I'd probably have been ready to get down on one knee.

But that's June. So beautiful it hurts your heart, with a husky
laugh and a wicked glint in her eyes. Looking at her reminds
me of those nights at sea with the navy, gazing up at a starry
night and feeling tiny and expansive, all at once.

She doesn't mean it, though. The smiles; the laughter. The
fact that I know this and I *still* want her makes me the biggest
idiot of all.

Harry has a ginger ale ready for June when she comes out
of the back room, the irate politician long gone. She picks it

up with a murmured thanks and weaves her way through the crowd, and though I expect her to find another bar stool, she heads for my booth instead.

She must've got something good if she's calling it a night already. I know better than to ask, but curiosity burns in my gut, and I mull it over as she picks her way across the floor. Is the politician sleeping with someone he shouldn't? Does he have some scandalous fetish, or secret dodgy donors?

A dusky pink sheath dress brushes against June's curves as she walks, the hem grazing her mid-thigh, and she's twisted her brassy hair up in a high ponytail since hiding away. The delicate slope of her neck draws eyes as she passes, and I'm already sliding back to make room when she arrives.

"That was quick."

June shrugs, dropping into the booth, pointedly ignoring all the eyes still tracking her every move. Does it get tiring for her, being watched like this all the time? It must do. But there's no strain on her brow as she slaps an old newspaper on the table, folded open to a half-completed crossword.

"He's an idiot. Didn't exactly make it difficult for me."

This is another pattern with June. Once she's done making fools of arrogant men, she likes to unwind with a ginger ale and an old crossword. I'd think it another carefully crafted behavior to charm her watchers, except apparently I'm the only one who finds this so cute I could howl. The first time I saw it, I practically had to bite my knuckles to keep from yelling how perfect she is.

"Eleven down." June spins the paper to face me, a pen balanced against her slender knuckles. "Since you're not working tonight, you can help me with this."

"Who says I'm not working?" I pluck the pen from her

fingers, the brief brush of contact sending my heart slamming into my ribs. Fuck, she makes me so tragic. "This place is my office as much as it's yours."

June levels me a flat look. "You've been scowling at me all night."

Shit. Busted. "Maybe you're my mark."

Or maybe she's right and I can't focus when June is in the room. Knowing that she's close and stringing some creep along for information—that sets my teeth on edge. I can never look away until I'm completely sure he's gone and she's safe, and even then, I make sure to walk her home.

On nights like this, June *is* my job.

Unpaid. Unacknowledged. Probably unwanted too, but her safety is more important than her liking me.

And it can't piss her off too badly because she's sitting beside me in this booth, so close the fabric of our clothes keeps brushing together. No body contact yet. I can maybe kid myself that I can feel her heat against my side, but this room's too muggy for that to be true.

"You gonna tell me what you learned?" I fill in the letters as we talk, my handwriting so much messier than hers. My letters score deeper into the paper, the ink thicker and more vivid. Hers are pretty and delicate, just like her.

June laughs softly. "Sure. For a price."

Yeah, that's what I figured. I wasn't really asking anyway, but one thing I've learned with June is it's better to be the one asking the questions. She deals in secrets, after all, and I'm full to the brim with my clients' confessions. Running my mouth would be a disaster.

To be fair, June never seems to pry with me. But maybe it feels that way for all her other marks, too. Asking the questions keeps me sharp. Keeps this safe.

"What did he want from you?"

June wrinkles her nose. "What they always want." She plucks the pen from my hand, finishing the answer I'm writing then moving to six across. Her ponytail swings over her shoulder, hanging against her front like a shiny rope. Her ginger ale sits untouched, moisture beading the glass and a wedge of lime half sunken at the surface.

And this is another reason I should keep my distance from June. I know for a fact that the things I think about her, the things I want—they're about as welcome as the mumps. I'm no better than that sleazy politician, panting after her and wanting to touch, to taste, to fuck. Wanting to claim all her beauty, to keep her all for myself.

"Don't you get tired of it?" I should stop pushing. I know I should. Because her shoulders are tensing, and if I keep going like this, I'll drive her away.

It would be a relief and a kick in the chest, all at once.

"Of course I do." June shoots me a glare, and it fills me with perverse pleasure. Those men she tricks for information, they only get her giggles and smiles. Me? I get the whole range of her expressions. More of the pissed off ones than any others, if I'm honest. "But I'm using the tools at my disposal. You told me you respect that, Marcus."

"I do," I tell her quickly, because it's true. I'm not shaming her, I just… I worry. "But I'm trying to picture doing it, and I can't see it. I don't know how you can stand those assholes for even a minute."

June huffs out a breath, but she's softened again. She fills in another clue, and she must have shifted closer because now her shoulder's brushing mine. So warm and smooth through the fabric of my shirt.

"It's just talking. But you couldn't do it, Marcus. You don't even smile for me, and we're almost friends."

"Yes, I do." Surely I smile for June. She's the only person I'm always happy to see. And what the hell does she mean by 'almost' friends?

She snorts. "No, you don't. I think I'd remember that."

… She would?

I lean back in the booth, the hubbub of the bar making my ears ring. I need this distance. This moment to collect myself. To remember that I can't trust June, and I can't let myself think this is real. That's how she does it—how she gets under a man's skin.

Some days, when my control's wearing thin and I want her so badly I can *taste* it, I think maybe I don't care. That it would be worth letting her play me for an hour or two of her sweetness. To bask in the warm glow of her smiles.

But my clients trust me with their secrets, and they're at risk here, not me. I clear my throat, shuffling along the booth, putting some much-needed space between our sides. June gives me a strained smile, and every part of me aches.

If this was real, I'd do anything for her. I'd offer up everything I am.

But it's not real, and this is the only part of June I can allow myself: a shared crossword, then a rainy walk home.

June

There are a handful of places in this city that I go to regularly. They're my usual haunts, the places where I'm all but guaranteed to find powerful men halfway down a bottle and behaving badly. It's a mix of bars, members' clubs, luxury hotels and casinos, but this one… this is my favorite.

It's a speakeasy. A relic from the twenties, complete with hidden entrances and art deco tiles; glittering chandeliers and plush velvet booths. Barely anything has changed with the place since it was a law-breakers' den, and the clientele are still about as trustworthy as rattlesnakes.

It's gorgeous. Sin and salaciousness, draped in shadows. Doesn't matter what night of the week you visit, it's guaranteed to be packed full of warm bodies, the air vibrating with voices and swing music. People tuck themselves in alcoves and slide their hands up skirts; they drink fancy cocktails and confess all their darkest deeds.

I learned to dance in this bar. My grandma taught me, back

when she ran the coat check. Lindy hop, charleston, blues—all of it. It comes in handy these days too, that's for sure.

A drink slides toward me across the bar, and I thank the bartender, wrapping my fingers around the cool glass. The fiery taste of ginger spreads over my tongue as I sip and I hum with pleasure, licking my top lip.

There are eyes on me. I can feel them like ghostly fingers on my skin, so I play it up, tossing back my hair then taking a long pull from my straw. And all the while, my eyes are fixed on the mirror behind the bar, scanning the crowd for a potential target.

I love bar mirrors. What a great invention. They're probably meant to make the room look bigger, or to give the bartenders a heads up about any funny business, but for me, they make my job a thousand times easier.

There.

My eyes flick to the corner of the room, drawn to a familiar set of vivid blue eyes. Marcus Miller leans against the speakeasy wall, arms folded over his chest as he watches me, his gray shirt sleeves rolled up to reveal his navy tattoos.

I swallow, my mouth suddenly dry, then take another sip.

He keeps watching me.

Crap.

It's not that I can't work with Marcus staring at me like that. Lord knows he does it often enough that I can tune it out, mostly. But on nights like tonight, when I haven't seen him for a few days and his attractiveness slaps me in the face all over again...

It's hard to concentrate. Hard to think about anything except the dream I had about him last night. One where it was *us* tucked away in a darkened room, the air thick and hot,

Marcus's big, scarred hands sliding up my bare thighs and his teeth scraping over my throat, his weight pressing me into a wall and squeezing the breath from my lungs.

Gritting my teeth, I fix my gaze on the bar. I can feel without looking that my nipples are poking at my dress. All it takes is a single thought about Marcus, and ping! My body's ready. Flushed and tingly and wanting. And damn, I'm trying to look tempting but I'm not hanging up a welcome sign. I slide off my stool before any of the men close to me can get the wrong idea.

Clutching my cool glass, I weave through the crowd, heading away from the bar, away from Marcus, away from everything. I pass by a raised platform, a live band playing under a shaft of golden light, the musicians' faces dewy with sweat and their eyes closed in ecstasy.

Where to hide in a speakeasy? I'm spoiled for choice, but those alcoves really are too convenient. I check a few before finding an empty one, then glance around me before slipping past the heavy red curtain.

It's dark. Hot. The air smells like dust, and my nose itches but I stay put, too relieved to be alone for a moment without anyone's eyes on me. Leaning back against the wall, I feel every uncomfortable part of my body: the bra strap digging into my collarbone, my sore feet from wearing heels, the lump in my throat, the raw ache in my chest from seeing Marcus. Every time I see him, it's like a scab tears off and I bleed all over again.

I want him so badly.

And he won't even let our shoulders touch.

"Crap." My head falls back with a thump, the thick curtain muffling the live music before it gets to me. Some of these alcoves have benches and chairs in them, but not this one. It's an empty dark space, but nothing more. Guess that's why it was unoccupied.

Okay. Slow breath in.

Slow breath out.

In.

Out.

Ice clinks against the side of my glass as I sip my ginger ale. I can do this. I can go back out there and dig up something worth knowing; I can ignore Marcus's scowl and act like he's nothing to me too. Like we're hardly better than strangers.

But that dream was so good. Marcus pushed his fingers inside me and called me baby.

"Stop it," I grumble, telling myself off as I hide in this glorified cupboard.

My head swims as I push upright again. It's too hot in here, too close, and I need to get to work so I can leave. My body's crying out for the long walk home, the cool mist of rain clinging to my skin as I stride through the dark streets.

I make it half a step toward the curtain before it twitches aside, a shadowed figure crowding into the alcove. The music blares louder until the curtain falls back in place.

"Occupied!" I blurt, my voice high and strangled. My shoulder blades press back into the wall.

"What the fuck are you doing in here, June?"

The tension gusts out of my body as fast as it came. I'd know that rumble of a voice anywhere.

"I needed a minute."

Marcus shifts closer, and I can make out his features now. He's scowling deeper than ever, his eyes indigo in the gloom. "Are you meeting one of those assholes? I can't watch you in

149

here. How the fuck am I supposed to keep you safe?"

I blink at the P.I. There's so much wrong with everything he just said, but I start with the easiest part. "That's not your job."

And it's not, however much I might like it to be. It makes sense now, though. All the staring. Marcus doesn't want me for himself or anything—he's designated himself my bodyguard. So freaking noble.

Well, I don't need a keeper. I focus on the righteous anger, pushing away the dull hurt. The disappointment.

"The fuck it isn't." Marcus folds his arms, muscles bulging, and I can't help staring at the tattoos winding around his forearms. There's an anchor, a swallow, a pattern of crashing waves. Shipwrecks and tentacles. "You dangle yourself as bait, but what happens if one of them catches you, June? What then?"

I don't want to hear this.

"I'm careful," I snap. "I never go anywhere alone with one of them."

Marcus spreads his arms wide. "You're alone now!"

God. *God.* I hate that he's right. I shouldn't have slipped in here, shouldn't have let myself get overwhelmed like that. I'm lucky it was Marcus following me in here and not someone else.

"It won't happen again," I tell him stiffly. "Alright? So you can stop watching me now. In fact, I see no reason for us to interact at all."

The silence that stretches between us is horrible. My gut twists and I feel sick, like I've been drinking something much stronger than ginger ale. And all the while, music pulses and the crowd chatters, the sounds seeping through the thick velvet curtain.

"You mean that?" Marcus's voice is guttural.

I shake my head, face crumpling. "No."

His arms come around me before I realize I'm crying. My hands shake so badly I slosh ginger ale down the front of his shirt, a dark strain spreading over the gray fabric.

"Shit! I'm sorry. I didn't mean to—"

"It's okay." Marcus plucks the glass from my hand and ducks down, placing it on the dusty tiles near our feet. "Come here."

As he gathers me against his chest again, my vision blurs. For an awful second, I thought maybe our hug was over before it started.

And this is *it,* surely. The only hug I'll ever get from Marcus Miller. I ball my fists in the front of his shirt and try desperately to commit every detail to memory. There's the hard swell of his muscles, so warm through his shirt. The thud of his heartbeat so near mine. Even the sticky damp patch I made on him, smelling like ginger and lime.

"I hate wearing heels all the time," I whisper, and I don't even know what I'm saying. When I'm around Marcus, it's like the roles are reversed and suddenly *I'm* the one confessing to stupid things. Out of control. "My feet really hurt."

Marcus grunts, then his hands drop, gripping the backs of my thighs. I barely know what's happening before I'm lifted, legs wrapping around his waist and the wall at my back.

My arms wind around his neck. Dangling in their heels, my feet throb with relief. "Um. Thank you."

Marcus huffs a laugh. "Anytime."

If only *that* were true. I'd never want to walk again if Marcus could carry me. I'd never sit on another chair if his lap was an option. And though I know he's just being noble again, I still sift my fingers through his dark hair where it hangs right above his collar. The pale line of his scar is ghostly in the darkness.

"Your hair is so soft."

"June," Marcus says seriously. "Are you having some kind of breakdown?"

I drop my forehead on his big shoulder, giggling wildly. "Maybe. Probably. I had the best dream ever last night, and it's thrown me for a loop. Now I can't think straight and you're *here* and I can't stop crying."

"What was the dream?" Marcus shifts me in his arms, resting more of my weight against the wall. I tighten my thighs on his hips, drawing him closer.

"You were in it."

The P.I can be so still when he wants to. Like a statue. "Was I?"

"Yeah. We were alone together. It was kind of like this. Except I wasn't crying or being weird and you were... you were..."

His hard chest presses against mine as he steps closer. It's heaving up and down, shifting with every breath he drags in, and his words are rough. Forced one by one out of his throat. "What was I doing, June?"

"Kissing me." God, why can't I stop talking? I'm such a blabbermouth. This must be how my marks feel, and let me tell you: I freaking hate it. Especially as I watch Marcus's scowl deepen and his face go cold and I still don't stop. "Touching me. You—you slid your hands up my dress, and then—"

"That's enough."

I nod, miserable. Marcus is right. I shouldn't say things like this to him. How much do I hate it when men get personal like this, telling me everything they want to do to me? It makes my skin crawl.

I pat his shoulder, aiming for breezy. "You can put me down now."

My feet ache even worse once I stand on them again. My drink is somewhere on the floor, but I don't want to bend over and scrabble around for it in front of Marcus. It's probably full of dust by now anyway.

The P.I watches me wipe the mascara from under my eyes with my thumbs, then smooth down my dress and fluff up my hair.

"You're going back out there." His voice is flat. "After that."

"This is my job, Marcus." Mine is twice as dull. And I hide my flinch when Marcus laughs, loud and grating.

"Yeah, no kidding. You nearly got me then, June, I'll give you that. A few more seconds between your legs and I'd have handed over my soul."

I don't know what the hell he's talking about and I'm sure it's insulting, but you know what? I don't care. I'm tired and achy and I threw myself at this man but he turned me down. I want to go home and sink into a bubble bath. I want to kick off my heels in favor of fluffy socks.

"Marcus?"

He steps aside to let me past. "Yeah?"

"Do me a favor, okay? Go screw yourself."

His startled laughter follows me out into the speakeasy, and it's warmer this time. More genuine. I don't care about that either.

I tried my best, but Marcus made the call for both of us. It's official.

He's none of my business—and I'm none of his.

Marcus

June is furious with me. If I couldn't tell from her pinched expression and tight shoulders, I'd know from the way she's been avoiding me every night. She's left four bars this week already, hopping down off her stool the moment she sees me walk through the door and disappearing with a swish of long, bronze hair.

It's fucking annoying. We both know she's leaving to work somewhere else, and how can I protect her when she treats me like a leper? Part of me wants to trail her through the streets, insisting that it's a free country and I can keep her safe if I want to.

But I know how she'd hate that, and I couldn't even blame her. If some asshole followed me around, I'd want to knock their lights out too.

It's mid-afternoon in Harry's bar on a Tuesday when I finally get her to talk to me again. Sunshine spills into the bar, filtering through the grubby windows, and the place is empty except for a couple of regulars. June's in a booth, her newspapers spread out on the table, chewing on the end of her pen as she frowns at a puzzle.

She looks different when she's off-duty. The changes are subtle, but they're there. Her sundress is looser and lighter, her hair coiled up and piled on her head, and a dainty pair of glasses perch on her nose.

"Hey, honey trap. You wear specs, huh?"

June stiffens when she hears my voice, my boots drumming over the floorboards as I stride closer. She looks so small in the booth, the cushioned sides swallowing her up on all sides, but she keeps her eyes trained on her paper like she didn't even hear me.

"June." She reaches slowly for her empty glass, stabbing at the crushed ice in the bottom with her straw. "June. Look at me for a second."

The way she sighs, you'd think I asked for some huge favor. An organ transplant, maybe, or a hundred grand loan. Brown eyes flick up to me, the same color as her favorite ginger ale bottles, and my heartbeat stutters.

"Marcus." Her lips press together. "Always a pleasure. If you want to hire me, you know my rates."

I snort, folding into the booth beside her, and her eye twitches with annoyance. Whatever. It *is* ridiculous. I find all the same dirt as her and she knows it.

"You can't avoid me forever."

Another stab at the ice. "Sure I can. It's a big city, Marcus."

"Not that big." It'd need to be a hell of a lot bigger to keep me away from her. Unless she says it outright, unless she orders me to stay away, I'm keeping June safe. End of discussion. "A little birdie told me something."

June shrugs, filling out her crossword clue with a flourish.

"Little birdies tell me lots of things."

She won't ask, but I'll still tell her. "Did you know that politician's been looking for you? Whoever you sold that tip to spoiled his image. Got him taken off that big project. He's put the word out, trying to find you."

He won't, obviously. No one in our world would ever hand June to a creep like that, but that's not the point. She needs to be careful. And I usually charge for info like this, but June huffs like I'm a pain in her ass.

"He put a call out looking for a tall blonde. He doesn't even remember what I look like."

I tuck my hands under the table, fighting the urge to touch her hair. "You could be dark blonde. Blonde-ish. Blonde adjacent."

June slides a different newspaper closer, switching to a new puzzle, her expression serene. "Then he'll need to ask for a blonde-adjacent woman. You and I both know the devil's in the details."

She's still barely looking at me. Avoiding my eye, stilted and tense and so clearly waiting for me to leave that I feel sick. How long will this go on for? All because I wouldn't let her play me like her other marks, using my attraction against me. I thought we respected each other more than that.

"June, listen to me." I lean closer, lowering my voice. Over by the bar, Harry's polishing a glass with a white cloth, his eyes dreamy as he stares at the wall. The faint strains of a baseball game play over a crackly radio, and cars rumble past in the street outside. "Whatever grudge you're holding, it's time to stop. Let it go. You tried to play me and it didn't work; I was pissed and you were embarrassed. If I can move on, why can't you?"

For fuck's sake. I was the one scraped raw for her entertainment. The one who's now haunted by the scent of her perfume, the feel of her warm weight in my arms.

Her fingers tugging at my hair.

Her thighs squeezing my hips closer.

Jesus Christ. Scratch that—maybe I am still pissed, because there's a good chance I will never recover from those minutes in the alcove.

I guess my mixed up moods are playing over my face, because June's finally staring at me, bemused. And I can't sit here for this, can't be a bug under her microscope, so I reach over and swipe her pen, scrawling my number in the margins of her newspaper, my face hot.

"Here's my cell. Ignore me if you want, but if you're in trouble, you call me. Understand? You call me and I'll be there. Save that number." The pen drops to the table with a clatter, and I shove my way back out of the booth. I'm too big all of a sudden, my limbs too long and so ungainly, and I can barely look at her as I stagger to my feet.

"See you, Harry." The old man raises a gnarled hand, waving as I stomp back out of his bar. The street smells like exhaust fumes and wet concrete, but it's still a relief after that quiet, sunlit booth.

Well. I laid it all out there. Gave her my number. Now it's June's move.

And if she doesn't call me... shit. I don't know what I'll do.

* * *

Part of me thinks June will *never* call, that she threw away my number, but three days later, she does. I've had my phone

157

within arm's reach at all times, the volume dialed up high like a grandpa so there's no chance I'll miss it, and I still jolt so hard I nearly swerve my bike into oncoming traffic. It's late, spots of rain glinting silver under the streetlamps, and I pull over quickly, my throat tight.

"June?" I scrabble my glove off, shoving my phone to my ear. I assigned her a special ringtone so I'd know it was her. "What is it? Where are you?"

The pause between my questions and her answer is the most agonizing stretch of time I've ever felt. I sit rigid on my bike, sick with terror, amped up with adrenaline. If that politician or some other creep got hold of my girl, I swear to god—

"I'm at home," she mumbles. She takes a shaky breath, then blows it out. "I probably shouldn't have called. It's silly. But I keep hearing noises outside, and something rattled my bedroom window, and I know you said to only call if I'm in trouble but I'm freaking out. Will you come over?"

I did *not* say that, but there's no time to argue. "Of course. Stay inside, make sure your doors and windows are locked, and I'll be there in twenty minutes. Do you have a weapon?"

Another shaky breath. "No. Or... I guess there are knives in the kitchen."

"Leave them there." If she doesn't know how to use them, they'll only make things worse. "Lock yourself in your bathroom and wait for me to call you. Don't come out for any other reason, okay?"

"Okay." Fuck. June's voice is so small. She sounds terrified, and I hate ending the call but I need both hands to drive. "Um. Thank you, Marcus."

"Don't thank me," I rasp. "I'll always come for you, honey trap. Sit tight. I'm on my way."

Marcus

Hanging up on her is the hardest thing I've ever done.

June

You'd think, considering the people I call friends, I'd be braver when someone creeps around my home at night. You'd think I'd be used to threats and weird noises and shifting shadows, but the truth is, I'm not like the other badass girls who make their living on the wrong side of the law. I'm a big scaredy-cat, and I freaking *hate* feeling vulnerable like this.

I chew on my thumbnail, staring at the bathroom tiles, sitting on the yellow, fluffy mat with my back against the bathtub. I locked myself in here like Marcus said, but it doesn't feel like enough. What if he doesn't get here in time? Or even worse, what if whoever is outside does something terrible to him?

Oh god. It would be all my fault, because I'm the wimpy idiot who called him here. I whip my phone out of my pocket, dialing another number. One for another friend who I can always rely on in a pinch, even though she sometimes makes the hairs rise on the back of my neck.

Anietta answers on the fourth ring. "Hello, pretty girl."

160

She always calls me that. I take a deep breath and tell her everything, spilling it all in a rush. She listens quietly, humming sometimes when I pause for breath, and as we talk, I'm unsettled and calmed in equal measure.

Anietta tends to have that effect. She's like a beautiful venomous snake: wonderfully soothing and hypnotic to watch, even as alarm bells ring in your head and your survival instincts scream to *get away.*

By the time I hang up, I've got two sets of reassurances. Two people coming to save me from my own chickenshit nature. So embarrassing.

I made Anietta promise not to hurt Marcus; described what he looks like just in case. She gave one of her smoky laughs and told me, "Of course I won't, darling. Pinkie swear."

I'm still relieved when he calls me again ten minutes later, telling me to come and let him in. My fingers are shaky, fumbling with the bathroom lock, and it takes me ages to creep through my apartment but the P.I. doesn't complain. He stays on the line with me, and when I finally open my front door, he ushers me inside and locks it behind us.

"Has anything else happened? Did you hear any more noises?"

"No."

His shoulders relax a tiny fraction. "Good. I checked the perimeter and the fire escape and the nearest alley, but there's nothing. Only some boot prints, and that could be from anything." Two steady hands grip my shoulders, and I melt into his touch. "June. You did the right thing by calling me."

It's like he can hear my thoughts. Can sense my rising embarrassment. Because if this was all for nothing, if I called *Marcus* and the city's best assassin to my apartment over nothing but a fox digging through my neighbors' garbage, I'll die of shame on the spot.

"Shit. I'm sorry."

He tugs me against his chest. "Don't be."

And god, I never thought I'd feel this again: his arms around me, his breath ruffling the flyaway strands of my hair. I bury my face in Marcus's throat and remember too late that I'm wearing pajama shorts and a crop top and nothing else. My bare skin presses against his clothes, cool and damp from the wind and rain, and he probably thinks this is another elaborate trap.

My heart throbs, raw and bruised.

Would he ever believe me? If I told him I love him? Sometimes it feels like I could spill my whole soul to Marcus and he'd still think it was a trick.

"Come on." He eases me back and takes my hand. Our fingers tangle together and my gut twists. "We'll check all the rooms together. Stay close."

Stay close. Sure. That's never been my problem with Marcus.

My problem is keeping away.

* * *

I live on the third floor in a pale stone building, the levels divided into eight apartments. After combing through my rooms, Marcus leaves and checks every single floor, knocking on my neighbors' doors and asking if they heard anything. I hover in my bathroom again, waiting for him with my arms wrapped around my waist.

I don't know if I'm relieved or sickened when the lady who

lives below me discovers someone knocked over a plant pot on her fire escape. At least I'm not crazy, I guess, and as Marcus relays this information, I find myself nodding. Steeling my spine.

Someone tried to break into my apartment. Sure. No big deal.

"Pack an overnight bag." Marcus drags me into my bedroom, yanking my ratty duffel bag from on top of the closet. I don't even have time to die inside about Marcus being in my bedroom, seeing my white and pink polka dot bed covers and the overflowing laundry hamper, because he's bossing me around, tugging open my drawers and rummaging through my clothes. "No, forget that. Pack for a week. You're not coming back here until the threat is gone, so bring everything you need."

He flings a fistful of balled up socks on my bed, the sleeve of his leather biker jacket creaking. Two pajama shirts follow, and a white cotton bra. Random handfuls of clothing rain onto my open duffel bag, and I stare at his broad back, white static buzzing in my brain.

He's *here.* He really came for me.

I wasn't sure he would.

Marcus is tugging my underwear drawer open when I finally jerk back to life.

"I've got it." I stumble forward, flapping him away. Lord, please don't let him see the giant granny panties I wear on my period. I sort through the tangle, only grabbing the cutest pairs, because apparently even in life and death situations I'm vain as hell. "I need to call around my friends, see if I can stay with one of them. Will you drive me there? Frankie crashed with me for a while last month so she'd probably take me in.

163

Or Harry might let me stay in his back room, or Anietta—"

"What are you talking about?" Marcus glares at me over his shoulder, stuffing my clothes into the duffel. "You're staying with me. It's the only way I can keep you safe."

I fall silent, choked by the sudden lump in my throat. For a man who refuses to trust me an inch, Marcus is very quick to bring me into his home.

The bedroom window sliding open makes us both freeze. Sweat breaks out on my palms and my chest seizes, and I'm so relieved to see Anietta's dark head poke inside that I burst out laughing.

Marcus stares between us, eyes wide. "June." He shifts slowly as Anietta pours herself through the window, putting his body between us as she slithers onto my bedroom floor. "Do you know who that is?"

"Anietta," I say happily. "She's my friend."

"June, I've heard of her. She's a fucking assassin."

"But she's not deaf," Anietta calls, shaking her head sadly. She hops up to her feet and extends a hand, a vision in leggings and a tight purple t-shirt. "Don't be rude, Marcus Miller."

I don't know what freaks Marcus out more—the fact that Anietta knows his name, or the handshake. He glances over his shoulder at me afterward, his jaw tight, and I bite my lip against another giddy laugh.

This night is so weird. I think I've felt every human emotion in the space of two hours, all of them dialed up to eleven. And now Marcus is standing in my bedroom, all scowly and manly and broad-shouldered, and Anietta is here too, sizing the P.I up like she's deciding where she'd slip the knife in first. Meanwhile, I'm clutching two handfuls of bright lace panties.

I step in between them. "Marcus is helping me out. I'm

going to stay with him for a few days."

"That's good."

"So stop looking at him like that."

Anietta arches an amused eyebrow. "I don't know what you mean."

Yes, she does. I mean he's *mine*. No stabbing or staring allowed, and that's final. And Anietta smirks but she must agree, because she leans against my windowsill, arms crossed. "Someone climbed up the fire escape."

Marcus grunts. "We know that."

"Do you know who sent them?"

I nod. "We have an idea." I tell her about the politician; about the tip that ruined his career and the rewards he's offered to get hold of me since then. Anietta hums and nods, then finally claps her slender hands.

"I'll take care of it."

Oh god. My eyes well up again, because I cannot handle people being nice to me like this. It messes me up. Twists up my insides. "Are you sure? You really don't need to. Oh, but I can't afford your rate—"

The assassin gives an airy wave. "Pro bono. You know I love you, pretty girl." She folds herself back through the window before I can manage a reply, melting back into the night.

I stand in silence for a long moment, head spinning and pulse tapping extra fast in my throat. Then I cross to my bag and shove my panties inside.

So. It's happening, though not quite how I always wanted.

Guess I'm going home with the P.I.

Marcus

How many times have I imagined bringing June back to my place? Too many to count. In my head, though, she always came willingly and not out of fear, her body pressing eagerly against mine and her hands tugging at my clothes. In some of my versions, we barely made it inside the front door before I lifted her against the wall, slotting my hips between her soft thighs. In others, she took my hand and dragged me to the sofa or the bedroom, pushing me down and climbing on top of me.

We were frenzied. Desperate for each other, knocking over lamps and sending shirt buttons pinging onto the floor. How else could I ever be sure that it was real?

Hey, a man can dream. Pretty embarrassing to think of now, though, especially as June tiptoes through my apartment, clutching the lapels of her coat like I might try and tear it off her.

She's barely dressed under that thing. Wearing the tiniest shorts and a crop top.

Fuck, her skin was so hot and smooth.

I clear my throat. "I'll put your bag in the bedroom." June blinks at me, eyes wide, and my next words taste sour. "I'll sleep on the floor. Obviously."

No way am I ruining my neck sleeping on my sofa, and besides, if I'm on the bedroom floor, any intruders would have to get past me to reach June. I'll be her tragic, pissed off guard dog.

"Okay. Thank you," she murmurs, tucking an escaped lock of bronze hair behind her ear, and some of my stewing anger boils away.

It's not her fault I want her so badly I can't think straight. She gets that all the time. Hell, she makes her living off it.

"I like your place," June says before I can move. I grunt and peer around my apartment, trying to see it through her eyes. It's only a few rooms, yeah, and the living room and kitchen are open plan, but the ceilings are high and you can see thousands of stars glittering through the big windows. And there's a lot of bare cement wall and exposed pipe, but that's fashionable these days, right? "You're cleaner than I expected," she adds.

Wow. Compliment of the century. I raise an unimpressed eyebrow, and June's cheeks turn pink. She rushes to keep talking, still clutching the edges of her lapels.

"Sorry! It's just—I've never seen a man's apartment before. Not in real life. And on TV, they're always so messy and gross."

Never?

Not even for…

Never?

"You take dates back to your place, then?" I cross to switch on a lamp as we talk, trying to act casual, but she's not falling for it. June huffs.

"Hardly. And I know what you're doing, Marcus, so stop trying to work me. If you want to know something, just ask me outright."

She's such a hypocrite. I fix her with a glare. "After all those times you flirted with me, June? After telling me about your little sex dream, trying to make me lose my head? Bit rich."

"I. Wasn't. *Working.*" June grits each word out between her teeth, stomping across the room and snatching her bag from my shoulder. She turns on her heel, her floral scent hitting me in a wave, and then she's gone. Marching around my apartment, trying doors until she finds the bedroom.

The door slams shut behind her, the noise echoing through the quiet.

I stand there like an idiot. Tension roils in my gut, and I can barely hear over my pulse thudding in my ears.

Because if that's true, if June has really been trying to coax me closer all these months, and I've done nothing but push her away...

"Fuck." I scrub a hand down my face, late night stubble crackling on my jaw. No, that can't be right. "Fuck."

* * *

"Are you comfortable down there?"

I shift against the floorboards, wincing at a knot in the wood. A squashy pillow cushions my head and a tartan blanket doesn't quite reach my feet. "Yes."

There's a long pause. A rustle of sheets as she rolls over to face me. "We can swap places."

"Go to sleep, June."

It's dark in here, and after an hour in separate rooms, the

tension between us has retreated to a low simmer. That's what we're like, the two of us. A pot heating on the stove, lid rattling and steam rushing, quiet for long stretches but liable to boil over at any moment.

What time is it? I've lost all track tonight. None of it feels real, especially with June here. When I glance up at the bed, her bare shoulder is unearthly in the moonlight.

"We could both sleep in the bed," she offers.

I swallow hard, chest drumming. "Not a good idea." The last thing she needs is to wake up with my cockstand digging into her ass. I'm not sure I'd survive that particular humiliation. Even now, just thinking about sleeping with my arms wrapped around her, my cock twitches and swells under the sheet, lengthening into the world's most miserable erection.

"Marcus?"

I sigh. "Yeah?"

There's a loaded pause. Then: "Um. Nothing."

I bury my face in my hands.

How long can we go on like this? Can I even keep June safe with all these messy emotions between us? My back pops as I push upright, the sheet pooling around my waist. I'm still hard, damn me, my cock pressing against the front of my boxers, and maybe it's wishful thinking, but I swear I can feel June's eyes trailing over my bare chest in the gloom.

"What were you going to say, honey trap?"

She squeezes the corner of the pillow. "I can't tell if you mean it sweetly when you call me that."

I frown. "Of course I do." Come on, I mean *everything* sweetly when it comes to June. "But what would you rather I call you?"

"Baby," she whispers, and I choke back a groan.

169

It's not real, I remind myself, the dismissal automatic. That's what I've always told myself in moments like these: that I'm falling under her spell, same as all those other suckers. That she's working an angle, about to trick all my clients' secrets out of me.

But June told me earlier the sex dream wasn't a lie. That she wasn't working all those times she flirted with me.

Fuck. I need to do it. I need to make the leap.

"Baby," I repeat, trying it on for size. June makes a soft little whimper, and god, I can't hide from this anymore. It's happening. It's so fucking real.

The mattress springs ping as June shoves upright, swinging her legs out of the bed. I barely have time to process her soft bare thighs before she slips down, straddling my lap, her arms winding around my neck. I spread a palm over her lower back automatically, the other braced against the floor, and I wince as her ass meets the rigid length in my boxers.

"Sorry," I grunt, but June sighs happily and grinds down against me. I clench my teeth, already seeing stars, and stroke up and down her spine. Up and down. Every time my palm moves from the soft cotton of her crop top to her bare skin, the blood pounds harder in my cock. "I've been an idiot about this, June. Haven't I?"

A breathless laugh. "Maybe a little." June guides my hand to her front, cupping her own breast with her fingers over mine. "I don't blame you, though. I would have been suspicious too."

She's so soft under my palm. Warm and perfect and thrumming with life. When I scrape my thumb over her nipple through her top, she moans and bucks into my hand, the bead hardening beneath the cotton.

"This is real, though." I know I should let it drop, but I need to hear her say it. Need to hear the words.

June does me one better. With an exasperated sigh, she grabs my hand again and slides it down the front of her shorts. My fingertips meet heat and slick, swollen flesh.

"Can't fake that," June murmurs, her hips rolling, encouraging my fingers to move. "Does that help?"

The air shudders out of me, then I'm squeezing her hip with one hand and rubbing her pussy with the other. Sliding my fingers between her wet folds, savoring her gasps as I nudge her clit. "Yes, it fucking helps. *June.* Baby, you feel perfect down there. So wet and warm. Sinking into you will be like sliding into a hot bath."

She laughs, delighted, and when I press one finger inside her, her head tips back and her hips lift higher. She starts rising and falling, riding my hand, the moonlight glinting off the shiny waves of her hair, and god, she's so fucking tight.

She's never done this before. It doesn't take a genius to work it out after what she told me earlier, and I know it's messed up, but possessiveness pounds through my veins at the thought.

Mine. My thumb circles her clit and June lets out a keening sound. I add a second finger and her hips slam down harder on my hand. *Mine.*

I'm gonna be everything she ever needs. I'm gonna leave her so well-fucked every single day that it never occurs to her to wonder about other men.

I shove her crop top up, sucking her bared nipple into my mouth. It's hard, so perfect as it nestles against the roof of my mouth, and June cries out, grinding herself down against my hand.

"Up." I release her nipple with a pop. She's wound tight already, and this is roaring along too fast. I want to drag it out,

171

want to savor June like a ten course meal. "Kneel up, baby."

She does as I say, her fingernails digging into my shoulders. Even in the blue-tinged shadows, June's dark eyes are unfocused. Hazy with pleasure. "Don't tease me, Marcus. Please."

"I won't," I promise, and it's like swearing an oath. On my life: I will never leave her wanting. I'd rather die. "But I want to taste you. Would you like that?"

June's breath catches, and then she's nodding hard, her lip drawn between her teeth. "Where do I...?"

After a quick glance behind me, I lay back on the floorboards again. The knot in the wood's still there, it's still hard and uncomfortable, but I'd cheerfully stretch out on a bed of nails for this. I pat my chest, staring up at the angel looming over me. "Up here, baby. Come sit here."

June

You know, I have dreams like this about Marcus at least once a week, so part of me wonders if I'm even awake. Surely I could never be this lucky. I could never have his big, muscled body beneath me, his bare chest dusted with dark hair, his tattooed arms flexing as he strokes up and down my thighs. His blue eyes watch me, so reverent, and the scar on his cheek is almost silver in the moonlight.

When Marcus pats his chest and tells me to sit on him there, I just about die on the spot.

What if I'm too heavy?

What if this *is* a dream and I wake up before the best bit?

I push myself to stand on wobbly legs and hook my thumbs in my pajama shorts, because if this is a dream, I'd better hurry things along.

Marcus lets out a winded noise as my shorts drop onto his belly. I step out of them carefully, then tug my top off for good measure too.

When I shuffle forward and straddle his broad chest, I'm

naked. Flushed and overheated, practically crawling out of my own skin.

"I feel…" I scratch my fingernails over the swell of the P.I.'s chest. He's somehow even bigger with his clothes off, packed with toned muscle and dusted with old scars. "I feel like there are thousands of fire ants under my skin. So tingly and squirmy and like—like if you don't keep your hands on me, if you don't touch me *everywhere,* I might explode."

Marcus's throat bobs, even as one of his big hands cups my pussy. Just covers it and holds it, like he owns it. "Then I'd better keep touching you."

"Yeah." My thighs shake as I crawl higher up his body. "You'd better."

I have a vague idea of what he's going for here, but I still squeak in surprise when he grips my ass, guiding me forward until my bared pussy hovers a few inches above his face.

Because god, I've never been so exposed in my freaking life. I bury my face in my hands, and I must be the color of a tomato from head to toe.

"Relax," Marcus says, like it's that simple. "It'll feel good, I promise." He kneads my ass as he talks, and okay, that is weirdly soothing.

I rock in his grip, peeking down between my fingers. "What if I suffocate you?"

Marcus barks out a laugh. "No offense, June, but I think I can take you. I'll tip you off if I need to, okay? But that won't happen. Besides…" He gets his old scowl back as he stares between my legs. "What a way to go."

My snort melts into a sigh as he lowers me down, his mouth surrounding my pussy. It's hot and wet and soft and gentle, and it's overwhelming and not enough all at once. I grip his bed frame beside me for balance with one hand, trying to keep still so I don't break his nose with my pubic bone or something.

Crack. Marcus swats my ass, the hot sting spreading over my skin. "Move," he orders, voice muffled.

Ooh-kay then. Such a bossy P.I.

I love it though, and I always have, and as I start to roll my hips, I'm thinking dreamily of every time Marcus has bossed me around. Giving me his number and ordering me to call. Telling me to be careful around my marks. Checking that I'm staying hydrated in hot bars, and insisting on walking me home.

I pluck at my nipples, head lolling to the side, watching Marcus through lowered eyelashes.

He watches me back, tongue stroking deep inside me.

It's always been like *this*, too. The both of us circling each other, staring intently, neither willing to make the first move, nor able to focus on anyone or anything else. The rest of the world fading away when the other is near.

When the men I trick for their secrets look at me, they see a pretty body. An empty vessel, completely non-threatening. But when Marcus looks at me, he stares into my freaking soul.

He's the only man to ever be wary of me. To not underestimate me.

Oh god, I love him so much.

My breath hitches, and my throat is tight, but I will *not* be the weirdo who cries during sex. I pinch my nipples harder, grinding down on Marcus's tongue, and he's *everywhere,* lapping at all my aching, tingly spots. The stubble on his chin rasps against my inner thighs.

"You taste so good," he rasps, the words vibrating through my clit, and that delicious buzz is what finally tips me over.

What makes my muscles lock and my breath seize.

I tense over Marcus, gasping and shuddering. The bed frame creaks under my grip, and heat flashes through me, and I'm coming, and coming, and coming. It drags out so long my ears ring, coaxed by Marcus's relentless tongue, and when after a short eternity I slide off him to one side, I'm made of jelly. I'm a puddle on the floorboards.

His chest rises and falls. He's panting, his chin slick.

"Fucking finally," Marcus heaves, a big hand clapping down on my bare thigh. For a moment, my chest pinches with startled hurt, but then I realize what he means—not that I took too long to come, but that the two of us took too long to get *here*.

Breathless and naked. Sticky and sweet.

I nod at the tent in his boxers. "Should I...?"

I've got no idea what I'm doing, but I've always been a quick learner, and I'm almost as eager to get my hands on Marcus as I am to feel his touch on me. But he must sense the exhaustion crowding my brain, must see my eyelids drooping, because Marcus shakes his head, then pushes to his feet with a groan.

"Not tonight. Come on, sleeping beauty."

I take his offered hand and force myself to stand. What the hell did he do to me down there? It's like I've never walked before. Like I'm a baby deer. My muscles are twitchy and wobbly, and I'm so wet and swollen between my legs that just pressing my thighs together makes me hiss.

What would it feel like if he fucked me like this? If he licked me into a wobbly mess, made me so sensitive I can't stand it, then slid that hard length inside me?

"Earth to June. You gonna sleep in the bed?" Marcus guides me to the mattress, flipping back the covers.

"Sure," I slur, crawling under the sheets. "If you sleep in here with me."

He snorts, tucking the blankets up to my chin. "You drive a hard bargain."

The mattress dips as he climbs in behind me. A strong arm wraps around my waist, hitching me back against his hard body, and I sigh happily, practically drooling on the pillow already.

"Do you think I'll be staying here long?"

Marcus pauses, burying his face in my hair. Then, so quiet I nearly miss it: "I hope so."

* * *

Anietta texts me over breakfast. It's mid-morning, shafts of buttery sunshine spilling through Marcus's huge windows, and I'm attacking a stack of pancakes like it's my mission in life.

The P.I glances over from the stove, a spatula in one hand and a dish towel tossed over one shoulder. He's thrown a gray t-shirt on with his black boxers, and it clings to his muscles every time he twists or reaches for something. Crap, why is that sight so hot?

"Is that your bloodthirsty friend?"

I blink at my phone, trying to parse the long line of emojis. She's sent me a poop, then a knife, then a skull, a ghost, a thumbs up. A dancing flamenco lady and an ice cream sundae.

"I think it's done. She's, um. She's dealt with the politician."

"You *think*?" Marcus turns off the stove and marches over, plucking the phone from my hand. A line forms between his heavy eyebrows as he stares at the emojis. "Is this some code I don't know about?"

"No." I shovel another forkful of pancake into my mouth, covering my mouth as I chew. "That's just Anietta. She's not a good speller so she prefers talking in pictures. Like hieroglyphics."

"Oh." Blue eyes dart to me, then away. We're probably both thinking the same thing: that if the threat is gone, there's no reason for me to stay here anymore. Our excuse is gone.

I wait for Marcus to tell me to stay another night just in case. He's always so bossy, but as the silence stretches, my heart sinks.

Was it a one time thing? Was I not very good?

Jeez, all I had to do was kneel there. How did I screw that up?

"I'll drive you home after we eat," he says, and it's like a door slamming shut in my chest. Ow. "I'm meeting a client this afternoon, and I need to do some prep."

That's all he says. Nothing about calling me. Nothing about seeing me later.

I nod, staring at my pancake stack. "Okay."

But how can I eat now with a lump in my belly? I manage two more bites, then shove my chair back, muttering something about taking a shower. Suddenly, I want all the evidence of last night off me. Wiped from my brain and from my skin.

Because it seems like we tripped straight from one miscommunication to another. He wanted something casual, and I...

I wanted forever.

Marcus

June's off with me again. I'm not surprised to find her in Harry's bar mere hours after dropping her home, but I *am* dismayed when she won't meet my eye. She's on her favorite stool at the bar, nursing a soda, and though it's early evening, she's clearly getting ready to work. Her hair's shiny and perfect, tumbling down her back in bronze waves, and her cream dress nips in at the waist and accentuates her curves.

She's so fucking beautiful. An angel in a beat-up bar.

I catch her eye in the mirror, but she ducks her head, playing with her glass. Spinning it slowly on the wood, crushed ice and lime bobbing in the pale liquid.

When some asshole in a tailored suit pulls up the stool beside her, my whole body aches. I want to slam my head against the wall. No, fuck that—I want to slam *his* head against the wall, then carry June out of here slung over my shoulder. Take her home and remind her that she's *mine.*

I slide into the nearest booth instead. Whatever I've messed up, I'll still look out for her, and I don't trust this guy. I don't trust any of the guys who come sniffing around June, and I guess that says a lot about me too.

"Evening, sailor." Harry's called me that ever since he saw my navy tattoos. He shuffles past my booth, carrying a box full of empty glasses and bottles. "You keeping an eye on June-bug?"

I grunt, staring at her back. That asshole's moving closer. "Always."

Even when she's pissed at me, I'll watch over her. And what the hell have I done now?

I didn't pressure her this morning to talk about us if she wasn't ready. Wouldn't let her touch me last night when she was too tired to make good decisions. I didn't even try and boss her into staying with me, though lord knows I wanted to.

I can't lick a girl's pussy once then demand a lifelong commitment. That's unhinged. I know that. But I've got this sickly, creeping feeling that maybe I could have. Maybe I *should* have.

If I did, would we be here right now? Sitting apart, the air tense between us? Or would it be *me* on that stool, sliding closer until our arms brush?

Fuck this.

I explode out of the booth, and I must look insane to the people clustered around the bar, but I don't care. I need to get to June.

"Excuse me." My words are polite, but my tone is not. I glare down at the tailored suit, one possessive hand gripping June's shoulder. I'm his exact opposite: broad instead of lean, tattooed instead of clean cut, dressed in jeans and biker boots instead of office wear. "You need something?"

The man's already glancing between us, recalculating. He shakes his head, sliding off the stool with his palms raised.

"No, man. She's all yours."

She's not a *thing*, damn it, not an item you can hand over, and even if she were, he's in no position to pass her off. The whole thing makes me so mad, makes me so tense and sick and seething, that I barely feel it when June hops down and grabs my hand.

"Come with me."

She's pissed off. It's clear from the set of her shoulders, from her snippy little tone, and I'm furious too, but our fingers still tangle together as she leads me into Harry's back room.

It's a small, musty space filled with squishy sofas and coat racks and a bookcase. A kettle and coffee cups, and the stack of old papers June combs through for her crosswords. It smells like old paper and ink, like stale coffee and the damp street outside.

She drops my hand as soon as we're alone, wheeling around to glare at me. "Marcus! What the hell is your problem?"

What is my problem? Now that's a million dollar question, and the answer starts and ends with the avenging angel glaring at me like she's about to conjure a lightning bolt. And I know I had no right to scare her mark off like that, but I can't sit through this tension between us for another minute.

We've done months of that. *Years*, even, and I'm done with it.

We're sorting this out. Right fucking now.

"I don't care about your work." I head that off before she can take us down that road, raising my palms. "I mean, I'll be honest: I don't love it. I get sick every time some asshole thinks he has a right to you. But I respect that you do it and you're good at it. As long as you let me protect you, that's fine."

"Okay," June grinds out, and her tone says it all: *Get to the point, Marcus.*

"But you wouldn't even look at me out there, and I can't go back to that, June. We came so far last night. Do you really want to take three steps back?"

Her shoulders slump. She looks so exhausted. "No." Her brown eyes are fixed somewhere in the center of my chest, on the gray t-shirt I threw on this morning after my shower. The shower I took with her in the next room, curled up in my bed. How the hell did we get here?

"But…" She wets her lips, and looks so fragile suddenly. It cracks me open down the middle and makes my hands twitch toward her. "But I, um. I misread things. I didn't want a one night stand or whatever it was, and I'm just, if we're keeping things casual, I need to protect myself, you know? I need to put up some barriers."

My boots thud against the worn carpet. I've heard enough, and June gasps as I crowd her against the wall.

There's a cork board behind her shoulder. As I press her against it, pinning her in with my arms, a postcard from Las Vegas slips on its pin, dangling askew.

"This isn't casual." Fuck. Even when I'd never touched her, it wasn't casual. I took one look at June and no other woman existed for me like that. "I didn't want to rush you, but screw it. Baby, you're *mine*."

June blinks up at me, her brown eyes wide, her lips parted, and I'm already yanking her dress up. Running my greedy palms up her thighs. The door's still half open, the sounds of the bar floating down the hallway, but I don't go to close it. Now that I've started this, a meteor couldn't make me pause.

"You can play those other idiots, but I need that settled, June. Say it. Tell me what I want to hear." I'm being so pushy, demanding things I have no right to, but she *likes* it. June sags against the wall, cheeks flushed, and she seems weak with relief. She's arching against me, rubbing up on me like a cat.

"I'm yours. I never want anyone else, Marcus. Ever."

"Good." June squeaks as I lift her, hitching her thighs around my waist. The cork board rattles against the wall. "Because I'm gonna give you everything you ever need."

Our movements are quick and choppy. We don't have time and privacy like last night—all we have is this burning need for each other, and it sets my teeth on edge. I all but snarl when she reaches between us, unbuckling my belt with shaking hands, and when she draws out my cock, it looks how I feel. Flushed and angry.

Not with her.

Never with her.

With every asshole who ever laid eyes on her.

I kiss June hard, reaching under her dress to yank her panties to the side. She's warm and wet, the moisture slick against my knuckles.

"Ready?" I'm shuddering with tension, a tendon standing out on my neck. I suck a harsh bruise onto her throat, breathing hard.

"Please." June squirms in my grip, trying to notch me at her entrance. "Now, Marcus. Do it. Please."

And I was right. Sinking into June is the sweetest thing I've ever felt. Even with her tight channel strangling me, even going painfully slow so she can adjust, it's everything I thought it would be. I skewer her to the wall, pressing my weight onto her, and the bite of her fingernails into my back is the best nip of pain.

"Oof," June wheezes once I'm all the way in. She's blinking

at the ceiling, brown eyes hazy. "You're—yikes. You're really big. You feel even bigger than you look."

Is that a compliment? Whatever. It takes every ounce of my control to hold still and grate out my next question. "Do you need me to stop?"

June shakes her head fast, her hair dancing and tickling my throat. "No. Oh my god, don't you dare. Just—just go slow to begin with. Okay?"

Obviously. I'm not a complete caveman. I want her to like this, damn it, to come away addicted to how good this feels, because now that I've felt the wet heat of her pussy, I'm going to crave it every damn hour.

We both suck in a breath as I draw out. Not far. Just an inch.

When I sink back in, June lets out a ragged groan.

"How's that?" I speak through gritted teeth, hips pumping between her thighs. June's wriggling against me, hips rolling to meet my slow thrusts. There's a deep flush crawling up her throat, and every time I push inside her, it goes a little easier. She's so slick, so eager, sucking me inside. "You like that cock?"

June whimpers and nods. "More. Give me more."

I speed up a little. Give it to her harder, thrusting deep in time with my heartbeat.

"You're so fucking perfect, June-bug," I grind out, borrowing Harry's pet name for her. I want to call her every sweet thing I can ever think of. Want her to try on terms of endearment like hats. "Do you have any idea how right you feel? Look at you bouncing on my cock. Taking it all like such a good girl."

June's moan is strangled. Her breath hitches, and I pump harder.

Yeah, she's a genius at reading people, but I can read *her.* I

184

know which buttons to press; which things she'll like. She'll see.

I'm going to turn this angel inside out. I'm going to scoop all the darkest fantasies out of her brain, and I'm going to ruin her for other men.

But first, I'm going to feel her come on my cock.

I palm her breast. Pinch her nipple and give it a rough twist, then reach between us in search of her clit as June shudders out sigh after sigh in my ear, turning her face to lick the salt off my neck. Our flesh slaps together, and I can hear myself grunting over the distant sounds of the bar.

It's base. Primal and shameless, and June's so wet that it trickles down her thighs.

"You're. Mine." I pinch her clit hard, punctuating my words with two hard thrusts, and June's thighs tighten around me like a vise. She comes with a low moan, and I feel her inner muscles twitch and flutter. Feel her clamp down on me, getting impossibly tighter, wetter, and hotter.

I wait until she slumps in my arms, boneless again with her flushed forehead pressed against my neck, and then I wedge myself deep and finally let myself go.

It *hurts.* Pain and pleasure and longing crackle up my spine, and I empty everything I have inside of her. The relief makes me lightheaded and I sway us against the wall, the cork board rattling, a pin dropping to the floor.

When I finally set her down, we're both mussed and sweaty. A line of white streaks down June's thigh.

"Be careful. Don't step on that pin." I grab a paper towel from Harry's coffee station, sending an inner apology to the old man as I kneel at June's feet, dabbing carefully between her legs. I clean every inch of her, taking my sweet time, and as her fingernails scratch at my scalp, my eyes drift closed.

My forehead thumps against her stomach.

She wraps her arms around my shoulders and holds me tight.

"This is it," I grate out. "We're all settled. I'm yours and you're mine. Right, baby?" I squeeze the towel so hard my knuckles ache, waiting for that final confirmation.

"Right." It's a single word, but it floods through my raw insides, soothing and cool. Above me, June laughs. "This is it."

I rock back on my heels and smirk up at my girl. "Well. We got there in the end."

June

ᘓᕷᘐ

F *ive years later*

I weave through the speakeasy crowd, my beaded dress brushing against my thighs. Eyes follow me through the darkened room, raking me from head-to-toe, and I hide a smile, smoothing the fabric over my hips.

Even now, years after giving up my honey trap work to partner in Marcus's P.I firm, I still preen automatically under the attention. It's powerful. A rush. It means I *could* dig up some juicy secrets tonight if I wanted, if I didn't have a more pressing engagement.

"Look at you." My husband meets me on the crowded dance floor, blues music pulsing around us, heady and slow. "Every person with a pulse wants you tonight." His shirt is open at the collar, braces looped over his broad shoulders. He came here from meeting a client, and he's got the savage glint of triumph in his blue eyes.

The meeting went well, then. That's good. That means the

tip I coaxed out of a corrupt businessman last week was useful.

Honestly, even if it wasn't, it was worth doing for the way Marcus bent me over a table immediately after. He appreciates my talents, uses them freely in our work, but he's always a little rougher with me afterward—in the most delicious way. Watching other men flirt with me frays his control.

"Did he go down okay?"

I left our son with our friend Tabitha. Or more accurately, with her responsible husband. "After some coaxing."

Marcus smiles, relieved, and tucks a lock of hair behind my ear. "The mark will be here in an hour or so. We've got some time."

The crowd twists and flows around us, moving in time to the throbbing music. It's hot in here, the backs of my knees already damp with sweat, but I grin as Marcus sweeps me into his arms.

He spins me slowly, our legs slotted together and his palm spread over my back. Our hands are clasped, my other arm draped over his shoulder.

"My grandma worked the coat check here. She taught me to dance," I murmur, pressing my words against his neck.

"Not like *this*." Marcus dips me to make his point, his muscles flexing as I sink down in his hold.

I choke out a laugh, swept upright again. Our legs press together, and my core aches. "No. Not like this."

We spin again, the low lights blurring. Marcus is everywhere, surrounding me, so hot and hard and strong.

Maybe we can find an empty alcove before the mark gets here.

"These look good." I flick a suspender, and he grins, stopping our circles. We stand in place for a moment, pressed together and rocking.

"A gift from Harry."

"That's sweet. I think they dated, you know. Harry and my grandma."

We fall quiet, but it's nothing like the strained silences that used to stretch between us. It's comfortable and heady. It's bliss. And as my husband dances me slowly across the floor, my chest is almost bursting with how much I love him.

I brush my lips against his ear. "Want to find a free alcove?"

Pressed against my front, his chest seems to swell. Marcus changes our direction, spinning us slowly toward the edge of the dance floor. "What do you think, June?" he rumbles. "I'm not fucking dead."

I throw my head back and laugh, blue and purple lights pulsing overhead.

Oh yeah, I'll get him in an alcove alright. Then I'll drop to my knees and show him *exactly* how good he looks in those braces.

IV

Blade

Description

The first time we meet, I put a knife to his throat.
Then he kisses my hand. So I follow him home.

Listen, I never meet guys in this city. Not ones that survive me, anyway.

And this man? He's magnetic. A trickster with eyes like liquid gold. After I nearly kill him, he bows like a gentleman and makes my tummy flutter.

So I follow the conman and scale his building, then slip through his balcony door.

He's already kissed my hand. I shouldn't be greedy.

But I want him to kiss so much more.

Anietta

I spend so many hours of my life hidden in musty closets. Seriously, you'd think the sorts of men I'm sent to kill would air out their fancy suits once in a while, but no. Tonight's clothes are as crusty as their owner, and as I silently stretch my limbs one by one in the corner of the closet, the scent of mothballs tickles my nose.

Screwing my face up, I fight the urge to sneeze and scowl at the dark closet walls, nose itching and eyes watering.

I won't sneeze. I never do. You think a stupid mothball would throw me off my game?

My target is three rooms over, hosting a poker game in his personal study. After snooping around this mansion for hours last night, I can officially say: money does not buy taste. There *is* such a thing as too much gold leaf.

I mean, I guess I wouldn't know. I spent years in a grimy studio apartment with a foldout bed and water stains on the walls, and despite making a name for myself in this city's underworld, I still only moved to a slightly nicer place four months ago. And I *still* haven't fully unpacked. Call it nerves—the constant fear that I'll blink and everything I have will melt away. For whatever reason, I've never truly settled.

But anyway, if I decked out my tiny apartment in red velvet and marble like this guy's mansion, people would come knocking for me to tell their fortunes.

Thump.

A muffled crash floats through the walls, followed by the tinkle of breaking glass and the roar of laughter. Yes, please laugh and joke together. Get rowdy and drunk for me. It can only help me if my target's visitors wake up with blurry memories. And if he comes staggering in here after too many drinks, already clumsy and vulnerable, even better.

I yawn, quiet as a cat, jaw cracking in the silence. It's hot in here, surrounded by the dark shadows of suit sleeves. Muggy and stale. I'm itching to stride out there and slit his throat at the freaking poker table, subtlety be damned, but that's the pins and needles talking.

What should I eat after this? I'm kind of craving falafel.

Another burst of savage laughter. That probably means a humiliating loss for some poor sucker, but whoever it is, I won't pity them. They're all the same, those men. Old and leathery, yet pawing after college-aged girls young enough to be their granddaughters. Tight-fisted and mean-spirited, calling themselves titans of industry when really they got lucky or were born to a rich name, then built their fortunes by bleeding everyone and everything else dry.

I'm not bitter. I swear.

But I won't lose a wink of sleep after killing this oil baron.

"Come on, come on." I tap one foot on the closet floor, arms crossed. With my eyes closed, my hearing feels even sharper,

195

until it's like I'm in the room with them. I can hear every thump of a glass against the table; every scrape of a chair and cleared throat. Even the soft, slithering noise of cards being shuffled—but that could be in my head. I have a very active imagination.

"Excuse me for a moment." It's a man's voice: deep and muffled by the walls. Is it him? A chair scrapes back, and there are murmurs of agreement before footsteps echo down the hall.

He's coming closer. There's a guest bathroom partway down the corridor, but the man strides straight past, his gait confident and determined. I slide the knife from the strap on my thigh just as the bedroom door hushes open.

Okay. I can kill the oil baron while he still has guests. As long as I keep things quiet, it'll mean that the house comes equipped with suspects. Eyes still closed, I listen to him walk slowly across the bedroom, floorboards creaking under his weight.

He doesn't move like I thought he would. I figured he'd be stiff and clumsy, hampered by drink and old age, but even from the closet, I can tell his steps are agile. He won't go down easily. That's alright. I only need to make this quick.

I don't want a fight. I rarely do. I just want to get this job done, then go eat some falafel.

A drawer rattles open at the oil baron's bedside. Probably needs his medication or something. I nudge the closet door open, stepping out into the dim room, my steps silent over the thick rug.

Why doesn't he turn the lights on? I flex my grip on the knife, slinking up behind the man bent over the bedside drawer. He's picking through the contents, his breathing steady in the silence.

It's not him. Not the oil baron. As soon as I get a good look at his shape in the darkness, it's clear—from the broad shoulders to the shifty behavior. The blade of my knife glints in a shaft of moonlight as I lunge, setting it against the stranger's jugular and purring in his ear.

"Hello, darling. You're not the man I'm supposed to kill."

There's a long pause. The man's frozen, shocked upright, his chest heaving as he vibrates with the effort of keeping still. One false move, and his blood will splatter the ugly wallpaper. It could only be an improvement to the interior design. Honestly, who wants hundreds of cherubs watching them sleep?

The man is very warm. A wall of lean, muscled heat. It spreads over my front as I press against his spine.

"I'm glad to hear it," the stranger murmurs at last. He has a nice accent. Irish, maybe. Whatever it is, it sounds like lit hearths and the patter of rain and shots of late night whiskey. I smirk at the back of his head, running my spare hand over his body as I search him for weapons.

"What are you looking for at his bedside?"

A very careful shrug. "Insight, I suppose. It helps knowing people's weaknesses in my line of work."

Mine too. But sliding my palm over this stranger's muscled form, I haven't found a weakness in this man yet, except maybe turning his back on the closet. And who can blame him for that? There's no way he's really here for the poker game, though.

"Your line of work," I prompt, taking extra care to pat down the stranger's firm ass. He splutters a shocked laugh, shaking his head without slicing his own throat. A delicate balance.

"I'm running a long con." My ears prick up. He'll admit it, just like that?

I don't meet many con men in my line of work. I don't meet many men at all except for the ones I kill, and those hardly seem to count.

"I don't suppose you'd let me finish the job? I'm closing it tonight."

I huff, my breath ruffling the hair on the back of his neck. It looks auburn, though I can't be sure in the gloom. An elbow reaches back, nudging me gently. "Call it a professional courtesy. This job has been months in the making."

A professional courtesy? I *do* like that. It makes it sound like I have coworkers, like I don't feel like the loneliest girl in this whole city on some nights. Even my fellow criminals tend to avoid me.

I guess the knives make them queasy.

"If you warn him about me, I'll kill you too."

A grunt. "Of course."

I chew on my bottom lip, knife still held to the con man's throat as I mull over my options. I could kill this man too and call it collateral damage; I could gag him and lock him in the closet until I'm done.

Or I could let him go. Show him *professional courtesy.* Every time I think those words, warmth spreads under my rib cage. A coworker? For little old me?

"What's your name?" the stranger asks suddenly.

This is where I should lie. Pull a name out of the air. It's only smart, because otherwise I probably will have to kill him.

"Anietta," I mumble instead like an idiot, a blush spreading over my cheeks where the con man can't see.

"Ah. *The* Anietta." Our heartbeats thump audibly in the

pause, mine fast, his slow. He's not scared of me at all, is he? "It's an honor to meet you."

He doesn't even sound sarcastic. Oh god. I don't know how to process this.

"I'm Flynn," he says, rounding out the interaction with zero help from me. My knife might be at his throat, but I'm the one having a meltdown back here. The hilt is slippery in my clammy palm. "I'm going to turn around now. Is that alright?"

I nod, because my tongue is stuck to the roof of my mouth. And Flynn must sense the motion, because he pulls my wrist gently away from his throat, then turns slowly to loom over me.

Gosh, he's tall. I'm surprised I didn't need a box to threaten him. I blink up at the first person who's ever seemed truly pleased to meet me, the knife I would have sliced him with dangling uselessly from one hand.

He's older than I expected. Mid-thirties, maybe, with sharp cheekbones and a feral glint in his eyes. Dressed in a ghostly white button-down shirt and dark pants, he looks like he'd be at home with those wrinkly old board men out there. Like he carries a briefcase and makes phone calls from the back of a glossy black car.

His voice, though? There's something rough about his voice. He hasn't quite sanded all the edges off it, not even for this act.

"Well, now." Flynn's teeth flash white in the gloom as he grins. "No one warned me that you're such a beauty."

Gah.

I croak a reply. "I think the blood splatters put people off."

His grin widens. And he's still holding my wrist, keeping my knife away from him, yes, but also tracing circles on my pulse point with his thumb. I know that he's a charmer, that

199

he clearly makes a living from manipulating people, but god, if he stares at me like that for much longer, I don't know what I'll do.

Kiss him, maybe.

Scale him like a building.

Tug on his dark red hair and beg him to say more nice things to me.

Because has any man ever looked at me like this before? With hungry eyes the color of liquid gold, roving up and down my body like he wants to swallow me whole? Like I'm someone to be wanted and not feared?

"You can finish your con," I hear myself say. I sound breathless, not like myself at all, and it only gets worse when he rumbles in approval, stepping closer. The line of his shirt buttons brushes against my front, and white static fills my brain. "I'll kill him once you're gone," I manage to add.

Those eyes twinkle down at me. "That's very kind of you, Anietta." I watch, dazed, as Flynn takes the hand still holding my knife and lifts it to his mouth, the blade bobbing in the air. Warm lips graze the back of my hand, his eyes holding mine the whole time as he bows over my knuckles like a gentleman. "Much appreciated," he says, the words vibrating into my skin.

Jesus.

It was barely anything, a whisper of a kiss, but my skin tingles and heat roars through my veins. I sway on the spot, mind fuzzy, pressing harder against him, and Flynn's mouth quirks like he's amused.

"Look at you, rubbing against me. You're practically purring, Anietta. You're a little murder kitten, aren't you?"

Yes. God, yes. I nod frantically, brain blank. No wonder those crusty old men lose all their money to tricksters like

Flynn—he took one glance at me and it's like he's paged through my operating manual.

Step one: Make a personal connection.

Step two: Say pretty things.

Step three: Give the first gentle touches I've had in years.

And bonus tip: smell really, really good. Like fresh air rolling in from the coast.

A burst of laughter from the other room brings me crashing back down to earth. We're in the oil baron's mansion; there are guests present. We're at work, damn it, and I need to get my head on straight.

"Go." I tug my hand back and slide the knife back into the strap on my thigh, Flynn's gold eyes watching the movement with shameless interest. "You'll draw suspicion otherwise."

He nods, but from the slow way he backs toward the bedroom door... it's almost like he's as reluctant as I am for this meeting to end. He tugs his shirt collar straight, rakes his hair back with one hand, and his gold eyes don't leave me a single time, tracking my small movements through the gloom.

"It truly has been a pleasure, Anietta." His voice is hushed, but I love how Flynn says my name. It sounds so musical in his accent. Lilting and lovely.

I nod, my throat too tight for me to say anything more, and then he's gone. The only thing left of him is the lingering warmth on my front, and the memory of his hard body taking my weight.

When the oil baron's bedroom door clicks closed, I let out a shaky breath, wrapping my arms around my waist and squeezing tight.

Oh god. Oh god, oh hell.

That happened.

How am I supposed to concentrate now?

Flynn

I realize she's following me as I stride down the train, a shape darting past on the platform outside. It's late, the carriage empty except for a few huddled drunks and exhausted shift workers, their earbuds shoved firmly in their ears. Silver streaks of rain flash past the dark windows like shoals of fish, and I wonder idly whether the pretty little assassin carries an umbrella.

The table I choose is far away from anyone else. There's an abandoned coffee cup and an old newspaper on one corner so I clear the area, brushing down each seat ready for Anietta.

The train doors rattle open. Ahead of me, she steps onto the carriage, already grinning, her dark hair twisted into a bun and speckled with rain. She's dressed all in black, her clothes close-cut, and there's no obvious sign of her knife. No blood speckles and not a single hair out of place.

Christ, but that was quick. Something told me I might see her again, but already? I barely left the mansion thirty minutes ago. We're still on the outskirts of the city, both in the trickiest part of our jobs: the getaway.

That's the danger with cons. Folks part with their money in an excited haze, but then their common sense kicks in. They start asking questions, though far too late.

I make myself scarce long before they change their minds. But still: this is the dangerous part. All the close calls I've ever had, they've come *after* I've closed a job, and with a briefcase full of cash at my side, I'm a walking target.

"That mansion was one of the ugliest I've seen." Anietta chats with me as casually as though we're discussing the weather, approaching my table and sinking down into a cushioned seat with a sigh.

If she plans to kill me, this would be a good place to do it. No one's paying us any attention, and the train security camera is clearly broken, dangling from a twisted cable at the end of the carriage.

"They're often like that." I tilt my head, trying to gauge her mood. Is she smiling because her job went well? Or because she's about to finish me off too and loves the chase? Or hell, is the assassin just happy to see me? Lord, I hope that's it. For more reasons than one. "Insecure old men who need everyone to know how rich they are. No one will shed a tear, even if you made a mess of him."

Anietta straightens, clearly affronted. Her pink lips purse, and her gray eyes narrow.

Fucking hell, Flynn. Don't aggravate the killer.

"That came out wrong." I raise my palms in surrender, though we both know if this tiny slip of a girl wanted me dead, I'd never breathe again. It's all for show, but it seems to mollify her. Anietta scowls and sinks back in her chair, and I push on. "I meant no one will mourn him. I know you're a professional, kitten."

I'm pushing my luck by calling her that again, but I can't resist. She *is* a kitten. An adorable, hissing little feline.

"I didn't kill him." She scratches a fingernail at the edge of the table, still grumpy. Lord, I wish she'd meet my eye. Every time she does, it's like an electric shock zaps through me. "I knew it might cause trouble for you, figured it might draw attention, so I decided to come back another day."

Ah, shit. She called off her job for me? In our world, that's a big fucking deal. The sort of thing you'd think twice about doing even for someone you'd known a long time. And meanwhile this girl knows me for five minutes then throws out all her plans?

"Anietta."

Scratch. Scratch. Judging by the way she's carving at the table, she's having second thoughts about that decision now. Her pointy little chin is set and her eyebrows are pinched.

"*Anietta.* Look at me." Maybe it's not smart to boss around the assassin, but when she blinks up at me with those wide eyes, I don't care. I reach slowly across the table, telegraphing my every move, and when I wrap her hand in mine, her fingers are cold.

"Thank you, sweetheart. You didn't need to do that."

Her throat moves as she swallows. She's gone quiet again, like back in the room. So still and cautious. "Uh. Yes. You're welcome."

The train jolts beneath us, drawing away from the station. Yellow street lamps drift past the window, faster and faster, the train juddering along the tracks, and I'm still holding her hand. She's still letting me. As her fingers warm up in mine, I can hardly believe my luck.

"Are you headed home?"

Anietta shrugs.

Okay.

"Will you let me walk you?"

She shakes her head this time. My gut sinks as she draws back her hand.

Well, what did I expect? I'm too old for her, I insulted her, and I've already cost her a job tonight. Of course she doesn't want me walking her home. Besides, knowing where she lives—that would require trust. And who in their right mind ever trusted a con man?

No one, that's who. And I can't even be bitter about it. As my Ma used to say, I've made my bed and now I can lie in it.

"Perhaps you'll text me, then." I pluck an old ballpoint pen from a nearby table, then gesture for her hand again. The fact that she gives it, that she lets me write my number on her skin, makes my heart drum faster. Maybe it's not too late to find someone to trust me. Maybe there's hope. "Perhaps you'll let me know when you get home safely."

As if she's truly in danger from walking home alone at night. Anietta *is* the danger, but she gives another shrug, staring at the number on her hand with bemusement.

It's not a no. I guess that's the best I'm going to get.

We sink into silence. It's not a long train ride into the city. Barely twenty minutes of shrieking rails and rumbling metal, the exhausted passengers slumped against the foggy windows. The few times we go through tunnels, plunged into darkness and thundering noise, I can *feel* Anietta still watching me. Staring across the table, her expression raw.

I can't read her. For once in my life, I have no idea what someone's thinking.

Jesus. And some people *always* feel like this. How the hell do they get anything done?

* * *

My apartment always feels lonely when I step through the door. Echoing and cold. I should leave a lamp on or something, maybe get a cat or a bird, but I never seem to get around to it. It'd be like admitting defeat, somehow. Like saying: *Yes, this is it for me. This is all I have to come home to.*

Fucking maudlin. That's the late night talking. I've always been a moody bastard after midnight, and when I was a teenager my Ma would get tired of my nonsense and shoo me to bed, telling me it'd all look better in the morning. She was usually right, too.

I shrug off my suit jacket and check my phone.

Nothing from Anietta.

Well, maybe she lives further away from the station than I do. Maybe she has bad signal and her text will take a while to come through. Maybe she stopped somewhere on her way home.

Or maybe she's not going to text me and I'm a tragic old fool.

"Get a grip," I mutter, tucking my phone into my back pocket before flicking open the top buttons of my shirt. Most cons require me to blend in with the city slickers, but I could do without the stuck-up clothes. I grew up in hand-me-down t-shirts and faded denim, and that's what I default to when I'm not playing a role.

With a few lamps flicked on, the place looks slightly better, filled with squashy furniture and draped with blue striped curtains. And even though I'm light years away from the house I grew up in, there are touches of it here in my would-be home. The bare brick on one wall is not so different from the flagstones that lined my Ma's kitchen, so cold in the mornings that three pairs of socks wouldn't keep your toes warm. And there were always fresh cut flowers on the scrubbed kitchen table, put out on Fridays every week like clockwork, so I keep that going here, too.

This week is yellow tulips. The lady at the market chattered to me as she wrapped them in newspaper, saying they used to mean hopeless love but these days they're supposedly more cheerful. I kept glancing at them the whole way home, feeling like the joke was on me.

Well, here's hoping. I could do with a change in my fortunes.

I brush the tulip stems with my fingertips as I cross the small kitchen to flick the kettle on. Does Anietta like flowers? Are her fingers cold again?

Ah, Jesus. Look at me, mooning over a gorgeous young woman who shrugged at me more than she spoke, kidding myself that there was something there. A spark. I always knew I'd crack, but I'd never have guessed that *this* would do it. A chance meeting with a beautiful assassin; having a knife held to my throat and a very confusing bodily reaction.

I'm not usually one for those kinds of antics. But with Anietta? That girl could do anything to me and I'd thank her for it. She could step on me and I'd send up a grateful prayer.

"You've lost it, O'Malley." I set out a mug quickly, my movements practiced as I fish a tea bag from the cupboards and fetch the milk. "Finally. Took you long enough."

My phone buzzes as I'm stirring the tea, steam curling from

the mug and misting my cheeks. I yank it out, the tea spoon clattering to the counter top, and frown at my screen.

Unknown number. Obviously.

Three emojis: a house, a tea cup, and a pair of eyes.

Heart thumping, I wheel around. Anietta leans against the kitchen doorway, lithe and sly, her hair damp and pale cheeks wet with rain. She smirks at my shocked expression, her ankles crossed and her shoulders relaxed.

"What the fuck." She winces at my outburst, back tensing, so I speak quickly. "I'm glad you're here! But also: what the fuck. I, uh. You took me by surprise, that's all." Casting around my suddenly smaller kitchen, I finally remember my manners. "Do you drink tea?"

She's here. She's really here. Fuck.

Anietta lifts one shoulder. She shrugs a lot, this girl, but I will get some preferences out of her even if it kills me.

"Would you like to try some?"

A nod. There. I turn and rummage in the cupboards, pulling out my best red china mug, one with no chips and a pleasing heft to it. Probably shouldn't turn my back on an assassin or arm her with heavy china and boiling water, but lord knows how long she stood there behind me. She could have killed me any time, and I suppose she still might.

"I came in through the balcony doors," Anietta murmurs, like she can hear my thoughts. "You should lock them when you're not using them."

Well… not if there's any chance of *her* coming through them again.

"I will," I lie.

After eliciting another shrug, I give her one sugar, the same as mine. And when she sips her drink, her slender fingers wrapped around the mug, a slow smile spreading over her face...

Fuck. That smile feels like a bigger win than the briefcase of cash left abandoned in the living room. I could punch the air.

"I have shortbread too," I offer, still caught off guard by her presence. I'm usually so smooth, so in control of every interaction, and this girl has broken all my rules and sent me into a tailspin. Instead of pulling her strings, guiding her in the direction I want, I'm lost. Scrambling to keep up, to not make a complete fool of myself or, you know, wind up dead. "Or if you're hungry I could whip us up something—"

"No." Anietta sips her tea again then smiles. "Thank you, Flynn O'Malley. I just wanted to see where you live."

Right. Because it's late, and she doesn't know me, and I'm acting like a lunatic. No crazier than her, I suppose, but still.

"Will you come again?"

Has a man in his thirties ever sounded so tragic? There's another shrug as she sets her half-empty mug on the counter. Steam still rises from the surface. She's really going already?

"Wait, Anietta." I cross to the table, face hot, but I'm determined. My hand hovers over the flowers as I pick out the best tulip, the one with the brightest petals, the straightest stem, then pluck it from the vase. "Here."

She takes it from me slowly, like I'm holding out a stick of dynamite, but the flush crawling up her throat gives her away. She's pleased. Another rush of triumph crackles through my veins.

Oh, I'm in this. I've never played a better game than trying to please this young woman, and I've always been a sucker for high stakes. So she could kill me? *Eh.* Lots of things could kill me. I'm a walking bundle of reckless choices, and my Ma always despaired at my chances. If she was still alive to see me romancing an assassin, she'd box my ears.

It's worth it, though. Because Anietta could also look at me like *this* again, like I've hung the fucking moon, her fragile expression so sweet that it punches a hole in my chest.

"I like flowers," Anietta whispers. "No one has ever given me one before." She clutches the tulip close, the rain pattering against the kitchen window. "Thank you."

Okay. Now we're getting somewhere. She likes flowers? *I* like flowers. It's a match made in heaven, and if she sticks around, I'll bring her a new bouquet every day. And if she gave me a chance, I'd kiss her hand again, but she's already melting back through the kitchen doorway. I barely make it to the living room in time to see her slip onto the balcony.

All in black, she blends into the shadows. I expect her to climb down, but she scurries up toward the roof. And somehow—I don't want to think about it—she sends a text at the same time, because my phone buzzes, and then two more emojis arrive.

A tulip and a shower of pink hearts.

I tip my head back and laugh.

This girl. This fucking girl.

Anietta

I still haven't unpacked the final boxes in my new place, but now I'm never home to finish the job. Over the last few weeks, I've had only a handful of destinations: my jobs, my favorite food trucks, and Flynn O'Malley's apartment. Or the surrounding area, anyway.

Sometimes, if he's home, I'll knock on the balcony doors and wait for him to let me in. If he's out, I slide them open anyway and wander around inside, since he laughs and refuses whenever I tell him to lock them. And sometimes, when I want to see him so badly that my heart's a bruised little lump but I'm too moody to make good company, I watch his apartment from the rooftops opposite, snacking on my food truck dinner and wishing I could be a normal person for once.

If I were normal, I could do more than shrug when he asks me out for a drink. I could knock on his front door instead of scaling his balcony. I could accept the flowers he gives me with more than stunned silence, a painful lump in my throat.

I keep them. Every single one. And as they've started to wilt,

I've pegged them one by one to a clothesline strung across my bedroom, drying them out so they'll last a while longer.

Tonight, I wedge myself onto a neighboring building's fire escape, a foil-wrapped bean burrito in one hand and my phone in the other. The lights are on in Flynn's apartment, the glow so warm and welcoming I can almost feel it in my chilled bones, and his curtains are all open. He's started doing that for me, too, since he figured out I've been watching. I'm glad about that, but I'm less happy that he's stopped walking around without a shirt.

The stars glitter overhead, muted by the city lights.

I send a text. A pair of eyes, a moon, and a taco since I can't find a burrito emoji.

Flynn replies less than a minute later. He's started texting all in pictures too, like he's learning a foreign language. I refuse to think about how sweet that is. I can't handle it.

Flynn: Cat. House. Flower.

He has new flowers to give me. I shift on my perch, the freezing cold fire escape numbing my ass. The burrito's still warm in its foil, crinkling in my grip, but already I regret coming up here where the harsh wind whistles straight through my clothes. I'm in a grumpy mood, yes, but flowers! Would Flynn really care that much if I'm surly?

Anietta: Flower. Heart. Snowman.

Ten seconds later, the phone buzzes in my hand, his name lighting up the screen. I accept the call after a pause, pressing the phone to my cheek.

"Hello?"

"Anietta, there aren't enough emojis in the world for this lecture. If you're cold, will you *please* get your beautiful ass into my apartment and warm up? I'll make you tea with extra sugars. I'll wrap you in blankets." I grin at my knees, teeth chattering, as he goes on, ranting and raving in my ear. "I'll heat up your taco for you. Hell, I'll order you ten more, I'll rent your own private taco chef, but for the love of god, will you please stop lurking on rooftops and come in here where I can take care of—"

He cuts off abruptly as I hang up. My knees crack as I stand slowly, then shake out my limbs, the wind tugging my hair.

Invitation accepted.

I tuck my burrito under my arm. It's way too big for just me, anyway. I ordered with my hungry belly instead of my common sense, but now we can share it. Half a bean burrito for a fresh flower. An even trade. See, Flynn O'Malley won't get tired of me with deals like that.

He's waiting on the balcony when I get there, arms folded. The icy breeze ruffles his auburn hair, and he watches me slink over the rail, his jaw set with disapproval.

"Young lady, if you hang up on me again while I'm talking shit, I swear to god—"

I interrupt him, laughing. "Young lady?"

"I swear to *god*—"

"You'll what?" I cock one hip, grinning, because we both know it's an empty threat. Even if I weren't ten times deadlier than Flynn, he'd never hurt me. He's the real pussy cat here.

The con man stares back at me, mouth twitching as he fights a smile. He's standing in the balcony doorway, blocking my path inside, and as we square off against each other, something crackles to life inside me.

My heart beats faster.

The air sizzles between us.

Blood pounds between my legs, heavy and slow.

I could take him. We both know it. But part of me wants that fight, wants to scrap with this much bigger man. I want to see how it would feel if he unleashed all his strength on me; if he put those muscles to good use. I want to wrestle and grunt and sink my teeth into his shoulder, and then I want to surrender to him and put all my trust in another person for the first time.

Instead, I raise my foil-wrapped offering. "You can share my burrito if you let me in."

There's a beat, and a series of emotions flicker across Flynn's face. Disappointment, bitterness, resignation. But he's nothing but charm as he steps aside, sweeping an arm toward the door. "How can I refuse an offer like that? Come inside, sweetheart."

Sweetheart. I like when he calls me that. It's almost as good as kitten.

It's like he really wants me here.

Like he really cares.

* * *

"Killed anyone fun lately?"

Flynn clatters around his kitchen making us tea, our burrito warming again in his oven. He's a whirlwind of motion, leaving cupboard doors and drawers hanging open then nearly walking into them; opening and closing the refrigerator door three times before he remembers to get the milk.

This is off-duty Flynn O'Malley. No-con-in-sight Flynn O'Malley. It makes his daily transformation to slick charmer all the more impressive, but I *live* for these snatches of the real man.

He's kind of a mess. I love that about him.

"Not really." I hop up onto the counter, my socked feet swinging. "Just a corrupt businessman and some slimy guy who was trying to off his elderly mother for the inheritance. That one wasn't a job, I just heard about it and killed him for free."

"Community service," Flynn agrees, dumping two heaped sugars into my tea the way I like it, then a much smaller spoonful into his. The metal spoon clinks against the china as he stirs. "No loss there, then. I'd rather have cut off my own arm than hurt my Ma when she was alive." He shoots a wry smile over his shoulder. "Not that I'd have a chance at her. She could be vicious, you know. Lethal with a whipped tea towel."

I nod like I know what he's talking about, and stretch out both hands to accept my mug.

Warmth seeps into my cold palms. Steam mists over my numb cheeks.

The first sip sends heat sliding down my throat, all the way to my belly.

"Ah, there she is." Flynn scratches my scalp like a cat. I buck automatically into his touch, cheeks flaming. "My murder kitten. No more lurking on cold rooftops, you hear? Just come straight inside. You know I leave the balcony doors open for you."

"I can't come in too much." The top two buttons of Flynn's shirt are undone, and I stare at the patch of skin they reveal. The hollow of his throat and the ridges of his collarbones. He's wearing moss green today, and it makes his gold eyes seem extra fae.

Underneath that slick shirt, he's a wild man. You wouldn't blink twice if you found him playing a lute in some ancient

216

forest. "If I get too comfortable, I'll never leave. And we both know I'm too scary for you to kick me out when you get tired of me."

His huffed laugh ruffles my hair. Flynn's still scratching my head, but slower now. Like he's massaging me, his fingers slipping between my black locks. "I'll never get tired of you."

He says it like a confession.

My turn to snort. "You *will*."

I'm not an idiot. Flynn may like me more than anyone else does, he may be more comfortable with me than anyone has ever been, but I can't get carried away. There will be an end to this, and if I'm not mentally prepared, it will ruin me.

Who am I kidding? Even if I see it coming from a mile away, it will still ruin me.

Flynn's fingertips rub at my scalp, easing my tension away as his low voice drifts through the kitchen. "Just come inside. And stay, okay? Stay as long as you like."

I nod, lulled into a daze by his touch on my head. The hot mug in my hands; the warmth of this kitchen; the rough, lilting voice of the man in front of me.

Stay?

As in… I could sleep here? Maybe on the sofa?

"You'll take the bed," Flynn says, affronted, when I dare to suggest such a thing. "You're my guest, Anietta. You'll let me wait on you hand and foot, and I won't hear a word of argument. That's how this works."

He's funny when he's bossy. His thick eyebrows pinch together, and his voice gets extra gravelly. It makes me want to thump my mug down on the counter and launch myself into Flynn's arms, but I only just got an invitation into his apartment. I don't want to lose it already.

"I'll sleep in your bed," I repeat slowly, turning over the idea in my mind. Would it be bad if I asked him not to change the sheets? I want them to smell like him.

No, I can't ask that.

Shit. I need to be normal. Normal-er.

"Thank you," I blurt at last, realizing the time for politeness is long past. But Flynn just grins at me, the corners of his eyes crinkling.

"Can't believe my luck," he tells me as he turns to check on the burrito.

Yeah. I know how he feels.

Flynn

Anietta stands in the bedroom and watches me change the sheets with a weird expression, still gripping her half-drunk tea. There's no steam rising off the surface anymore and it must be lukewarm by now, but she keeps carrying it around, cradling it against her chest.

"You don't need to do that," she says for the third time as I bundle the sheets and toss them to the rug. I pull a fresh set out of the drawer, sniffing them quickly to check for mothball smell. I know she hates that, but we're good. Daisy-fresh.

"Nonsense." I toss the sheets onto the mattress and go to work on the pillows. "I'm going to make you comfortable, Anietta. So comfortable you'll forget to ever leave. That's my cunning plan."

My tone is light and she rolls her eyes, but I'm not fucking joking. That's my whole play here.

You know, it's good that I'm unprepared, because if I'd thought about this for too long, I might not have had the guts to offer. Having Anietta here overnight, soft and sleepy and

219

tucked up in my bed? Seeing her bleary-eyed and rumpled in the morning? Knowing that she's *close*, so close that maybe if I lay silently on the sofa once she's in bed, I might hear her slow breaths through the walls?

It's going to fuck me up. I know it.

Because I'm a con man. I'm not built to do the noble thing, and in this case the noble thing is staying far, far away from Anietta. It means keeping my greedy mitts off that beautiful young woman, and appreciating the scraps she's already given me.

But lord, I wasn't born to just take what I'm given.

I'm a liar and a thief, and I *always* want more.

"Flynn?"

She's staring at me, a concerned frown on her face, because I've gone rigid. Looming over the bed like a weird statue, strangling a pillow in one hand.

"If you've changed your mind, it's okay," Anietta says quietly. "I won't be angry or make a scene." And she looks even smaller than before, hovering in the center of my bedroom with one arm wrapped around her waist. Her cooling mug of tea is clutched right over her heart.

Fucking hell. Anietta is a killer, yes. Outright lethal.

But she's unaccountably delicate too. Like a vivid, poisonous flower. Not for the first time, I'm hit by the eerie realization that I could *hurt* her if I'm not careful. I could do some serious damage; I could tear her delicate little petals.

"I will never change my mind," I vow, with no hint of humor for once in my life. "I'm going to keep you and treasure you and love you until you're sick of me."

Shit. That last bit came out without permission, and now I'm hot under my clothes. Flushed and itchy and embarrassed.

But Anietta softens again, and the humiliation is worth it.

Sure, I'll confess all my deepest longings to cheer her up. I'll throw myself under that train. What else am I good for?

"I'll make us more teas," I mutter, even though we only just had some. It's a nervous habit, something to do with my hands and my mouth that doesn't include pawing at Anietta like a wild animal. "Make yourself at home."

She lets me leave without a word.

Fuck. I'm making such a mess of this.

* * *

I can't sleep. It's no surprise, not with this lumpy, too-short sofa and the crick in my neck and the restless energy humming through my body. Knowing she's near, my muscles are twitchy and my skin is hot. I'm extra sensitive, feeling every brush of my t-shirt and pajama pants as I toss and turn.

Too fucking warm. I throw off my blanket, and it lands in a muddled heap on the living room floor, the distant sounds of traffic rumbling on the street far below.

It's dark in here, but the city lights seep behind the curtains. They cast strange shadows from the potted plants and tinge the darkness blue, and I squint around my living room, trying to see it through Anietta's eyes. Is this the kind of place she'd like to live? Would she make changes? Would she like more books or a bigger TV?

What if I made her some kind of assassin's hobby area? A poisons lab or a knife throwing station. Would she stay then?

"Jesus Christ." I dig the heels of my palms into my eyes, flopping back against the sofa cushions. "Get a grip, O'Malley."

A small sound drifting from the bedroom makes me freeze.

221

I lay still, heart thundering and mouth dry, desperate to hear it again.

There.

After several long minutes, when I'm busy telling myself I must have dreamed it, must have conjured it with my sheer longing… it comes again.

A soft, broken moan.

Holy hell. I spring off the sofa like a jack-in-the-box, pure adrenaline spiking in my blood. And even though my heart's slamming loud enough for the neighbors to hear, my footsteps are careful and quiet as I pad down the hall.

I shouldn't go nearer. I should leave it alone, but I am not a good man. And I want Anietta's moans more badly than I've ever wanted any riches before.

Pausing outside my own bedroom door, I shift my weight carefully, mindful not to let the floorboards creak. Inside the bedroom, sheets rustle. There's a heavy sigh, and a hiccuping moan.

Slowly, so slowly, I rest my forehead against the door, sick with longing.

Would she welcome me in there? Or would she be horrified? I suppose I should be most worried that she'd literally kill me, but it's the thought of that horror that keeps me rooted to the spot.

Another moan. Fuck, I shouldn't listen to this. Turning to leave, the lump in my throat is sharp. Painful.

But then: *"Flynn."*

It's so soft I almost miss it. Because she's not calling to me; she's lost in the haze of what she's doing. Tossing and turning in my bed, touching herself and saying my name.

The bedroom door swings open under my palm. I'm not

thinking anymore; I'm moving on instinct.

She whispered my name.

Now I want her to scream it.

Anietta

Flynn O'Malley's bed is soft and warm, the mattress firm enough to soothe my aching back. As soon as I lie down in the tangle of his sheets, his scent hanging in the air, I'm done for. The faded band t-shirt I borrowed is baggy, swamping my body and pooling over my curves, and my nipples stab into the fabric like they're desperate to feel more.

They are.

I am.

I can't get enough of this. Flynn's bed, his clothes, his fresh coastal scent all around me. Knowing he's so close, and he likes me enough to let me sleep here, and having three empty tea mugs lined up on the dresser from his endless deliveries—I love all of it, and it hits my system like a drug. Makes me giddy and free.

It's instinctual, the way my hand drifts down my stomach. The way my palm smooths over the jutting bone of my hip before my fingers dip between my legs. And I'm only thinking of one man, one set of wicked golden eyes as I touch myself, breath catching and moans slipping from between my lips. My fingers swirl faster, the ache growing low in my belly.

God.

What would Flynn say if he knew I was doing this? Touching myself in his bed? He'd tease me, probably. I can hear the rough edge to his voice in my mind, can see the filthy glint in his eye, and I pinch my nipple hard, imagining *his* hand there.

Would he be rough with me? If anyone ever dared, it would be Flynn.

Would he take over, knocking my hands aside, or would he stand and watch, pretending to be cool and imperious? Making me finish what I started?

"Flynn."

His name escapes me in a hiss, and my hips buck up against the air. It's cool in this room, the air thick with shadows, but my skin is fevered. I'm glowing like an ember in the center of the bed. The sheets are kicked down by my ankles, my borrowed t-shirt slipping and sliding over my restless thighs, and when the bedroom door creaks open, I could weep with relief.

"Flynn?"

"I'm here, kitten." He moves quietly through the gloom. He and I, we're forever sneaking up on each other in the dark. But there's no glint of a blade this time, only the creak of the floorboards under his feet.

He comes and stands over me. Stares down at me, just like I thought he might.

"What on earth are you doing to yourself, Anietta?" There's that teasing lilt to his voice, and I might be embarrassed if each word were not thick with lust. I squirm on the mattress, pushing two fingers inside me.

"What does it look like, O'Malley?"

The shadowed form above me tilts its head. "It looks like a fucking sight for sore eyes, that's what."

That's the only warning I get, then the bed dips under Flynn's knee. He moves quickly, straddling my waist, and snatches my wrists, pinning them to the pillows by my head. My slick fingers shine in the moonlight.

If anyone else did this, I'd gut them. I'd leave them to bleed out in a crimson puddle.

But it's my con man, the man I've been yearning for night after night, so I buck up against him, whining shamelessly for his touch.

"Easy. Easy, now." Flynn hushes me, gripping both wrists in one big hand, then strokes a sturdy palm down my front. He traces down my throat, my chest, the length of my stomach, pressing down gently the whole way and pinning me harder to the bed. And I arch under his touch, so wet and aching between my thighs, blood pounding in my clit from where I started something then cut off part way.

"I need… I need…"

I can't put it in words, but Flynn chuckles. It's a filthy sound, and it makes me thrash underneath him, ears ringing.

"Oh, Anietta. I know exactly what you need."

* * *

What I *need*, according to Flynn O'Malley, is his shirt yanked off and tossed over his shoulder, his muscled chest ghostly in the gloom. What I *need* is his approving growl, low and deadly in his throat, as I rub against him.

I couldn't agree more.

And what I *need* is his roaming, shameless hand, touching me everywhere and pinching my nipples, laying claim to me like it's his right.

It is. Everything Flynn wants from me—it's his.

I've never trusted anyone like this before. Kind of funny that I've chosen a con man.

My pulse pounds in my skull as he lifts my hand with its slick fingers. He stares down at me in the dark, so big and primal and heavy, and his chest heaves as he sucks them clean one by one. His mouth is hot and wet, his tongue swirling around my knuckles, and holy *shit*, I've forgotten my own name.

There was a reason I wasn't going to try and do this with Flynn. Why I wasn't going to push my luck. What was the reason again? It's bobbing the back of my mind, swallowed up by ocean mist.

My other hand is still pinned to the pillows, his arm muscles flexed as he holds me there. The heat rolls off my con man's chest and washes over my front, taunting and tormenting, and if I don't get some freaking relief soon, I'm going to howl.

"*Flynn.*"

A rough chuckle. "Alright, sweetheart. Hold tight." The bed creaks again, his body shifting, and the weight suddenly disappears from my wrist. My hand jerks up automatically, suddenly free, but I force it back to the pillow where he left it.

"Good girl," a voice rumbles from near my belly.

Oh, wow.

I am very much *not* a good girl, I am a blood-soaked criminal with stalker tendencies, but when he says it like *that*… it's all I want to be. Flynn O'Malley's good girl. His kitten.

"Will you let me lick you up, Anietta? Will you let me taste

227

between your legs?"

I nod frantically in the darkness. Is it not freaking obvious?

"Yes. Do it. Hurry."

Another laugh, and this one vibrates through my core, because he's dipping his head, hot breath misting over my clit. I'm already tingling. Already rocking against the air. Flynn presses my thighs wide and I let him, my breaths quick and shallow, and when the slick heat of his tongue drags along my seam...

I lose my freaking mind.

"God!" Soft hair slips between my fingers and I yank at him, my obedience already long forgotten. My hips buck against his face, and I roll my whole body, undulating against the slide of his tongue. "That—it's—oh my *god*."

He responds by plunging his tongue into my pussy. Two big hands squeeze my ass, lifting me higher off the bed, tilting my body so he can lick deeper, *deeper,* and my feet kick as my eyes screw shut.

I'm glad it's dark. Glad he can't see the tortured grimace on my face, because this feels so freaking good that I almost can't stand it. It's so much pleasure, it's nearly pain. And beneath my racing pulse and fevered skin and sparking nerves, my heart is a raw lump in my chest.

I've barely been touched before. Barely exchanged more than a few sentences with a man before Flynn O'Malley, and now *this*? Flowers and sweet teas and shared bean burritos? Rolling around in Flynn's bed with his short, messy hair tickling the insides of my thighs?

Two thick fingers replace his tongue inside me. It's a stretch at first, a slight burning sensation, but even that I like, especially when his tongue laps at my clit over and over, so rhythmic as my head spins.

It's too much. I can't—I can't *think* straight—

"Flynn," I gasp, and he grunts with satisfaction as the shudders start in my thighs. My whole body begins to twitch with the force crashing over me, the pleasure and heat flooding my body in waves, and I squeak. It's too soon, I wanted more, wanted to drag this out for hours, but it's clear from the merciless way he keeps licking me that I never stood a chance.

I bow off the mattress, taut and shaking and damp with sweat.

When I collapse back onto the bed, Flynn finally lifts his head. His chin is slick and shining in the moonlight, and his gold eyes watch me, hungry and intent.

"Did you like that, Anietta?" It rasps out of him, like his throat is tight. Like *he's* the one who just got turned inside out.

"Uh-huh." Can't do words. Can't even nod. I can only lie here, boneless and ruined. I should return the favor, should do *something* surely, but I'm so overwhelmed I can barely breathe.

Flynn rolls to one side, flicks the hem of my borrowed t-shirt back over my thighs, then crawls up the bed and collapses beside me.

"Don't send me back to that sofa, sweetheart. I promise to behave if you let me stay. And if I snore, you can always cut my throat."

I laugh, but it's half-hearted. He's joking, right? Surely he knows I'd never hurt him. "You can stay if you don't hog the covers."

Flynn draws a cross over his heart. "Scout's honor."

Even though I'm the one who just came so hard spots floated before her eyes, Flynn falls asleep in less than a minute. His steady breaths huff through the bedroom, his chest rising and falling as he sleeps, one arm tossed above his head. And I lie here and watch him, mouth dry and chest aching, feeling all tangled up and raw though I can't figure out why.

Dawn seeps into the room at 5am.

I know because I watch it, still wide awake.

Flynn

⸺⟨℘⟩⸺

I've never slept so well in my adult life, and to be clear, Flynn O'Malley is an Olympic-level sleeper. I can sleep on command, crammed into tiny airplane seats or standing up leaning against train luggage racks. I sleep through neighbors yelling and sirens blaring; I can drift off in bright light or the muggiest heat of summer. Never let it be said that this con man suffers from a guilty conscience, because I sleep like a fucking *babe.*

But napping next to Anietta? Cozied up with my beautiful killer?

Forget it. I think I just extended my lifespan by three years.

"Jesus, Mary and Joseph." I borrow one of my Ma's old phrases, my voice thick and words blurry when I wake. Scrubbing at my face, I check the morning breath situation before wincing and rolling to face her side of the bed. "What a cracking night."

Pale gray eyes watch me, unblinking and exhausted.

Shit. If I've just had the equivalent of a spa retreat, Anietta looks like she spent the night in hell. Her dark waves are in disarray; she's shrunken and lost in the sheets. She might as well have passed the time shivering on that rooftop after all, she looks that wrecked. Purple shadows cling beneath her eyes, and her cheeks are ashen and pale.

"Anietta? You doing okay, kitten?"

Silence. Still no words, not even a blink. Only that exhausted, thousand-yard stare, her plump cheek smushed into the pillow.

"Okay." I'm clumsy, fumbling to sit up, my rusty morning brain grinding into gear as the morning light spills through the window. *Deal with this, asshole.* "Ah. Okay. Did I snore and keep you awake? Did I…" I trail off, swallowing hard before I complete my next god-awful thought. "Did I cross a line last night? Did I make you unhappy, Anietta?"

She seemed so into it. She called me closer; she begged for my touch. Did I misread that? God, I'll die if I did.

Pale lips purse. There's an eternal pause, and then finally, *finally*, a minute shake of her head.

And thank fucking god for that, but I can't linger on the relief for long, because it still doesn't explain this. Somehow, since dropping off to sleep last night, I managed to fuck up the best thing that ever happened to me. And that's classic Flynn O'Malley—of course I dropped a clanger somehow while I wasn't even conscious—but if I don't even know where I went wrong, how can I fix it?

"Tea," I offer desperately, clinging to the only certainty in this life. "Shall I bring us some teas? And fix us some breakfast? And maybe then you can tell me what's wrong?"

Anietta puffs out a tiny sigh, and her bottom lip wobbles. It fucking *wobbles*, her eyes suddenly swimming with tears, and

Jesus Christ, my chest is a smoking crater.

"Sweetheart," I croak, lost for all other words, and when Anietta's face crumples, I fall on her. There's no grace, no consideration. I watch that pain spread over her features, and I'm helpless to do anything except lunge for her.

"Flynn!" She's all pointy elbows and a shocked, raspy voice, wriggling against my iron grip. Crushed against my chest, I can feel her heartbeat racing near mine, and strands of her hair are somehow in my mouth, but I'm not moving away. Not yet. "Flynn, what the hell!"

"Talk to me." I grind the words against the crown of her head, hands roaming over her back, rubbing what I hope are soothing circles through the old t-shirt she borrowed last night. And as I touch her, she stops wriggling at last, melting slowly against my chest, my own ragged heartbeat steadying in response. "Take pity, Anietta. I'm an idiot when I first wake up, and this is too important for me to get wrong. Have I hurt you? What's happening here?"

A pitiful sniffle drifts up from somewhere near my collarbone. A damp patch is spreading over my chest, and god, that guts me to the core.

Still no words from Anietta, though. And cold, oily dread is spreading, seeping into my limbs.

"Have you changed your mind?" Those words taste so sour, but I spit them out anyway. It's important she hears this. "You know there's no pressure, right? If you've changed your mind, that's okay. You can still stay here. We can still be friends—"

Anietta's breathing stops. I feel it against my neck, and I'm in such a rush to keep talking that my words all muddle together. So much for the charming con man. "If that's what you want! Only if that's what you want. You can also leave and never speak to me again, or you can go back to snooping on me from rooftops, or you can stay here and let me hold you until you feel better. Whatever you want, kitten. Whatever makes you happy."

I'd give my right arm to be the thing that makes Anietta happy, but I don't say that out loud. This situation is messed up enough already.

When she finally speaks, it's so quiet that I almost miss it. "Flynn?"

Cotton sheets rustle as I shift her closer. She's cold in my arms, so slim and limp and fragile. "Yeah?"

A hoarse whisper. "I think I'm going crazy."

Well, that's two of us, but I don't tell her that. No, for once in my life, I don't crack a damn joke. I hold her tight and kiss the top of her head and wait for her to explain.

"I couldn't sleep." When they come, her words are stilted and unsure, and I rub her back like I might coax them right out of her. "I just lay here all night, watching the shadows move across the wall, and all I kept thinking was you'd wake up and you'd see me still here and you'd wonder why I hadn't left already in the night. Why I didn't get the hint."

I stiffen.

"What hint?" Because I dropped no such fucking hint. I'd rather poke my own eye out than suggest she should leave. "There was no hint, Anietta. I didn't want you gone. I *don't* want you gone. Waking up to you is the best feeling in the whole damn world."

I mean every word, but she's shaking her head, her hair ruffling against the stubble on my chin. "You can't mean that. I'm creepy, Flynn! Everyone gets freaked out around me, even my best friends. People who really know me, they keep me at arms' length. They never really let me in. Because I'm creepy and a killer—"

"And I'm a con man," I interrupt. "There are no angels in this apartment, Anietta, let's be clear. But sure, most people are scared of you. And those same people wouldn't trust me an inch. Can we blame them?"

A damp laugh warms my neck, and I squeeze her gently, grinning into her hair. I'm doing this. We're fixing this. It'll be alright.

"Can we blame them, kitten? Those are survival instincts at work. But it doesn't matter what all those other people think. Because I'm not scared of you, bloodthirsty little scamp that you are, and you seem to trust me at least a little. Don't you?"

This is not about me. I will not make this about me.

But I could sing out with relief when she huffs and nods. "Of course I trust you."

"Well, then."

It's not a clever argument. I'm still groggy and stupid from the morning, and Anietta is still half-deflated in my arms. But at least we're lying together now, our limbs twined and our body heat mingling. At least we're sharing this moment, raw though it is, and I think she gets what I'm saying.

Nothing and no one else matters. Not when I have her.

"Flynn?"

I grunt, rubbing my chin back and forth on her head. My stubble crackles over her silky hair. "Are you going to give me another heart attack, Anietta? At least let me have another tea first. One final cuppa before I go."

Sharp fingers pinch my ribs, and *that's* how I know she's feeling better. With a dramatic sigh, I roll my whole body weight on top of her, crushing her into the mattress, and this was a bad idea, because now I can feel everything. The jut of her hip bones; the softness of her belly; the swell of her tits. Her heat and the rapid pulse tapping in her throat.

Jesus Christ. My body wasn't truly awake before, but now it sure is. I shift my hips, but not before she feels my hard length digging into her thigh.

"Ignore that." Lord help me, I'm a grown man blushing over an erection.

Especially when a dark eyebrow quirks beneath me and a small hand slips down my front, cramming between our bodies to explore. "Are you sure?"

"Fuck. No, I'm not. Crack on, Anietta. Oh but wait, wait—"

She looks stricken for a heartbeat as I roll off her again, stumbling out of bed on shaking legs, but I hold up a palm, speaking over my shoulder as I stagger to the door. "I'm coming back, but I haven't kissed your mouth yet, have I? Just your pussy. And I'm sorry, but there is no way on god's green earth that the first time I kiss you is with morning breath. You can pout all you like. There's no fucking way."

Her soft laugh follows me into the hall.

It sounds like hope. Like relief.

Anietta

F lynn O'Malley scowls at the mirror while he brushes his teeth. As such a sunny man, the expression rests oddly on his face, and I tuck this secret knowledge of him away with the other tidbits I've collected over the last few weeks. Things like his messy morning hair and the way his cheeks crease when he smiles. Things like the pleased hum he makes after the first sip of tea, and the way he paces his strides down the street to avoid the cracks in the pavements.

Things like his favorite t-shirt to sleep in: a soft, heather gray.

And, as of last night, things like the hushed, heavy breaths of his sleep.

I've been like this for weeks, collecting pieces of Flynn O'Malley like a magpie stealing bottle caps. And part of me always figured that someday soon he'd get tired of me, that he'd send me away like everyone else does, and then I'd have nothing left but my bottle cap details to survive on for the rest of my lonely life.

But as I stand at his side, bare toes curling against the chilled bathroom floor, brushing my teeth in sync and watching Flynn O'Malley in the mirror... I'm not so sure. Maybe there isn't an end date on this one after all. Maybe it could last.

It's a terrifying thought. Scary but exhilarating—like how I imagine jumping out of a plane must feel. Sparks are crackling through my veins, and I swear I'm electric.

Flynn cranks the faucet on, bending over to spit into the sink. He's thrown a t-shirt on too, and now we almost match. We're both dressed in his softest, comfiest clothes; we both have rumpled hair and pillow creases on our cheeks.

We look like an ordinary couple. A pair of everyday lovers you might pass in the street, and automatic panic claws at my insides, because I don't *get* things like that. I'm not allowed them. Am I?

Flynn nudges my arm, straightening up, his mouth wet as gold eyes watch me in the mirror. "I can hear you hyperventilating back there. Don't freak out with toothpaste in your mouth, sweetheart. It's not good for you if you swallow it."

Ooh-kay. I bend over and spit obediently, ears ringing. Then his palm smooths over my shoulder blades, and I nearly melt into the bathroom tiles right here.

No one ever worries for me. They don't look after me or take care. The few friends I *do* have are great, obviously, but they don't fuss over me. They don't coddle, and it turns out I *like* to be coddled.

Because Flynn's a fusser. He always makes sure I'm warm enough, bringing me blankets and thick pairs of his socks. He had a spare toothbrush ready for me, and when I raised an eyebrow, he proudly showed me the box of tampons he bought weeks ago in case I ever visited during my period. The sight made my eyes burn.

"Are you hungry?" he asks now, still rubbing my back. "What do you fancy for breakfast?"

I rinse my mouth, rolling my eyes at the white porcelain. If he thinks I've forgotten his promised kiss, he's insane.

"I make a mean hash brown–"

Flynn breaks off as I straighten and spin to face him, my borrowed toothbrush clattering into the sink. I catch a glimpse of surprised pleasure, his eyebrows lifting, and then I'm *on* him, my front plastered against his and my arms wrapped tight around his neck.

He's so tall, I need to rock onto my toes to reach his mouth. But Flynn's a gentleman, and he bends down to meet me partway, a hungry groan tearing from his throat as our lips slam together. We're starving for each other, nipping and licking and sucking. It's a morning feast.

"Jesus," Flynn grinds against my mouth, big hands roaming over my back, my sides, my ass. His tongue slides against mine, then retreats, and I chase after him, our mouths both so minty. "You're a fucking firecracker. Be careful, Anietta. I'll need a pacemaker if you keep this up."

I have no idea what he's rambling on about, but I think it's complimentary. He sure seems approving as I brace myself against his shoulders and jump up, my thighs wrapping around his waist.

Two steady hands cup my ass, kneading my cheeks as Flynn holds me up. Every inch of me that touches him is burning up, hot and restless and tingly.

"See, this is better with fresh breath. Say I'm right, Anietta."

I nip his chin. "You're right, Flynn O'Malley. You are such a wise, clever man."

He groans, choking out a laugh as he spins us to the bathroom wall, pressing my back up against the tiles. With his weight leaning against me, I'm pinned in place, whimpering and arching against him. "I know you're talking shit, but I love it. God, I thought I was a better man than this."

"You're the best man." The *only* man in my eyes. Even with his forgetfulness and his funny knitted sweaters and the filthy way he looks at me sometimes. Especially with those things. And if it's praise he wants from me, I've got plenty of nice things to say, and none of them are lies. "You're all big and muscly and every time you touch me I get so wet—"

"Jesus fucking Christ." Flynn rocks against me, the hard line of his cock pressing against his pajama pants. I'm not wearing any panties, and that thin layer of fabric is the only thing between us. The only thing stopping the broad head of his cock from sinking where it belongs. "You're killing me. Stop. We've found my kryptonite: I'm a needy bastard."

Flynn's not needy. Or if it's needy to want love and compliments and nice, warm things, then I guess we're both basic bitches, because every time he calls me beautiful, happy little sparks explode in my chest.

"Can you feel it?" I don't know who this girl is, saying these things. Tilting her hips and squeezing him tighter with her thighs, encouraging to thrust her harder against the wall. Whoever she is, she sounds way more confident than I feel. "Can you tell how wet I am through the fabric?"

Flynn groans again, and that's quickly become one of my favorite noises. I'm going to play it over and over in my head when I'm alone. I'm going to draw it out of him every chance I get.

"Yes. Fuck. You're soaking through to me, sweetheart." A broad forehead drops against mine, and his skin is just as flushed. Just as feverish as I feel. "Do you want me? Anietta, do you want me inside you?"

Yes. God, yes. I want Flynn O'Malley as deep inside me as he'll go. I want to suck him into my body and keep him there forever.

"Do it." I scrabble at his clothes, tearing uselessly at his t-shirt. Should have undressed him before I climbed him like a tree, and Flynn huffs a laugh before reaching between us and tugging his waistband down.

Yeah, that'll work. Who needs to get naked? There'll be time for all that stuff later. Hours and hours of lying together, exploring each other's bodies, working up sweat after sweat. Right now, there are more urgent concerns—like how if I don't feel Flynn pushing inside me in the next thirty seconds, I'll scream.

"Okay?" We share a swift kiss, then his forehead is back against mine. And he's *there,* prodding at my entrance, the head of him thick and smooth, sliding against me in an agonizing tease. "Are you ready, Anietta?"

I puff out a breath. "If you don't fuck me this instant, I swear to god—"

Flynn bears down on me, leaning his full weight into the cradle of my hips. And it burns, stings so much my eyes water, and I'm about to say something when he eases back, fucking me with shallow, soothing thrusts.

"Easy." He kisses my cheek, my eyelid, the tip of my nose. "Try to relax, sweetheart. There's no rush."

Okay. Relax. I can do that. Because the second the thick length of him pushed inside me, my whole body tensed up, fighting the intrusion. But I *want* him here, I want to feel him stretching me, and remembering that helps. I soften, arms winding tighter around his neck, and Flynn hums, his thrusts still gentle.

"Ready for a little more?" Even now, he's coddling me. God, I love him so much.

I nod. "Yes. Keep going."

This time, he presses in further, and the stretch doesn't take me by surprise. And when I'm not fighting it, it feels… *good.* So freaking good. That burn is delicious.

"More," I mumble.

Flynn grunts, fucking deeper inside me.

And I feel it all in such minute detail. Every nerve ending in my body has sizzled to life, and I feel *everything.* The thick length of him splitting me open; the slick slide of our bodies; the hammer of his heartbeat against my front. I don't know what I expected from sex, but in my imagination, it was never this… this *visceral.*

I feel Flynn O'Malley in every inch of my body. From the tips of my toes to the roots of my hair.

"More," I beg again, and now he's really fucking me. Burying his whole cock inside me with every thrust, the sound of our flesh slapping together echoing off the tiles. The noise makes me giggle and Flynn chokes out a laugh too, sucking a kiss on my throat before burying his face in my hair.

"I never said this would be graceful, kitten."

It's not. I don't care.

Because it's so much better than that. It's perfect. Especially when Flynn juggles me in his grip, resting me more fully against the wall, then jams a hand between us, his clever fingers seeking out the places he licked me last night. Color glows high on his cheeks, and his hair is still messy from sleep, and the sight of his gold eyes glazed with pleasure makes my heart throb.

A pinch to my clit makes me hiss and buck harder.

Flynn grins down at me, savage promise in his eyes.

"Oh, we'll explore that, Anietta, don't you worry. I'm going to find every single thing that makes you tick. I'm going to work you into the ground, figuring out all the best ways to make you come."

"Promises, promises," I gasp. My head is spinning.

And when I seize up, it's with his thumb on my clit and his tongue on my throat. His name on my lips and his cock wedged inside me, and spots floating before my eyes.

"Anietta," Flynn grits out, and then he follows me over the edge. We cling together, slumped against the bathroom wall, my legs twitchy and shuddering, his wet heat pulsing inside my body. We're both tensed, our teeth gritted against the waves of pleasure, and when we both remember to breathe again, relaxing with twin gasps, mint laces the air.

"A shower," Flynn says, decisive. He sets me down on wobbly legs, and I watch him in a daze as he reaches over the tub, cranks the shower on and tests the spray as it warms. "A shower, and then breakfast. And then round two. Yes?"

Gold eyes flick back at me, cunning and lovely. I nod, mouth dry. "Yes."

No shrugs here. I've never been more sure in my life. I want this, and I want breakfast and round two, and I want Flynn O'Malley. Every inch of him.

"Will you shower with me? Can we do it together?"

His sharp laugh bounces off the tiles, and Flynn yanks his shirt over his head. When he emerges from the fabric, he's grinning. "Ah, Anietta. Is that a real question? You couldn't keep me out of there, love. I know you're terribly scary and all, but I've never had much self-preservation. Just promise not to brain me with a shampoo bottle."

I purse my lips, fighting a smile. "I promise. For now, anyway."

If Flynn trusts me, that's his business. And I sure as hell won't prove him wrong. Just like I've never been surer than when I'm placing my trust in the con man.

Maybe everyone else is right to keep their distance from us.

Doesn't matter anymore.

Flynn

ive years later

I realize she's following me as I walk through the flower market. Stalls line the edge of the docks, bursting with leaves and bright petals, and sellers call out prices and flower names, making themselves hoarse to be heard above the crowds. On the edge of hearing, water laps against the dock walls, and the early morning sunshine is buttery and warm.

So much for her surprise flowers. I roll my eyes, hiding a smile, and stroll to a nearby stand of roses, hands thrust in my pockets.

"Single stem," the seller calls from his spot nearby, wrapping a sold bunch of roses in newspaper. "Red, white and yellow roses. Handpicked bouquets."

I nod and offer a polite smile. Wait for the buzz in my pocket that I know is coming.

Sure enough: *bzz.* I pull out my phone, heart tripping even after five years. I *always* get tangled in knots when my wife texts. I'm like a pining teenager, and it only gets worse the longer we're together.

Anietta: Rose. Heart. Eyes.

Come out, little kitten. She'd have made herself known already, but she worked a job last night. She's cagey, sometimes, about coming to see me straight afterward. Like it might finally change how I feel about her. Complete nonsense.

Flynn: Cat. Knife. Heart.

I pause for a long moment, glancing at a nearby churro stand, the scent of cinnamon and warm sugar in the air. Then I add a donut emoji. Close enough.

Five minutes later, Anietta's voice rasps next to my shoulder. "The red roses. They're more romantic, don't you think?"

I wave at the seller, glancing down at my rumpled, murderous wife. "If you say so, my little killer. Lord knows I'd never argue with you on the job."

Anietta rolls her eyes, grouchy but pleased by my teasing. It reminds her I'm not afraid of her, and I never will be. "Shut up, Flynn."

We eat our churros leaning against the dock wall, chewing slowly and watching the sunlight glint off the water. As Anietta dunks her last churro in the melted chocolate dip, I trace a fingertip over the small swell of her stomach under her customary black top.

"You'll take time off soon, right?" I hate telling her what to do, but when it comes to this, I might actually have to dust off my bossy voice. "Your job is dangerous, sweetheart."

Anietta snorts. "Not the way I do it. They never even know what hit them."

I level her a look. And Anietta huffs and rolls her eyes, but

I can tell that she's pleased. She likes when I fuss over her, which is perfect, because I love to fuss.

"If you take time off, I'll wait on you hand and foot."

"Flynn."

"I'll rub your swollen pregnant lady hooves."

"Flynn."

I watch her steal my last churro, my cheeks aching from mirth. I'm only teasing her. She's perfect. This is perfect.

"I'll take time off," Anietta agrees at last, frowning at the water. "But I'll get bored. I'll be hanging around you all the time. I hope you're ready for that, O'Malley."

"Ready for that? Kitten, that's my dream. Why do you think I knocked you up in the first place?"

A sharp elbow digs into my ribs, and okay, I deserve that. It's worth it though, to hear her husky laughter.

Watching the morning light on the water, I don't know how a bastard like me ever got so lucky. If my Ma saw, she'd never credit it.

But I'm not an idiot. Anietta is my stray kitten.

And I'll *never* lock those balcony doors.

* * *

Thanks for reading the Sweet Little Sinners! I hope you liked them :)

For another sweet & steamy series, check out the Prickly Pear Springs! Starting with Dear Diary: *It's been three years since I confessed my love to my English teacher—but my heart still did somersaults today when I saw him at work.*

And for a bonus instalove story, grab your copy of Ride or Die. *She's sweet and innocent—and that's like catnip in this strip club. It's okay, though. I won't let the pretty bartender out of my sight.*

Happy reading!

xxx

Teaser: Dear Diary

It's him. Mr Finch is in the library—*my* library. Prowling across the lobby like Heathcliff across the moors. He looks exactly the same as he did three years ago, except the lines of his face are a little harder. There are more creases at the corner of his eyes, too, but he's dressed the same as always, with a gray button-down shirt tucked in at his trim waist, the sleeves rolled up his strong forearms.

When he glances at the help desk, Mr Finch jolts with surprise.

I crush the order form I'd been reading in my suddenly sweaty hands.

"...Emma?"

Should I be glad that he recognizes me? That the man who so callously broke my heart remembers my name? I suppose it's less humiliating than being completely forgotten, but right now all I want to do is run and hide.

"Mr Finch," I rasp, my throat so tight. "Um. Hi."

The Grumpy Grandmas are shooting us dirty looks for talking across the lobby, so I should be relieved when my old English teacher walks closer to the desk, dropping his voice. I *should* be.

Mostly, I just want a sinkhole to open up beneath the library and swallow me whole. Goodbye, cruel world.

"What are you doing here?" he asks, a deep scowl etched on his face. Like I'm stalking him or something. Asshole.

I mean, it's been *three freaking years.* And yes, I still think about him all the time. Yes, the mere sight of him has punched all the air from my lungs and made my nerves tingle. Yes, my body is responding to his closeness even now, a flush crawling up my chest and a low ache settling below my belly button. But I haven't been trailing after him like some desperate weirdo, thank you very much.

Believe me, when my teacher turned me down like that, so cold and dismissive, I heard him. Message received, loud and clear.

Slamming a paperback down on the help desk, I scan it aggressively, drawing a loud beep. This one's already been checked back in, but I need to make a point. "I work here, Mr Finch."

He turns to stone, a dismayed statue in the library lobby, and a petty side of me enjoys it. Yeah, he wants to do his class project here? Well, I was here first, buddy, and I'm an adult now. He can't boss me around or make me feel small.

"Every Friday?"

Dread laces his words. Good.

"Yup." My smile is not warm. "Like clockwork."

Scrubbing a hand down his face, my old English teacher gusts out a sigh. Now that I'm seeing him up close, he looks kind of tired. Not sleepy, but more... worn down by life.

Jeez, he's not *that* old. Mr Finch needs to get a hobby.

"The school schedule is already set." He bites out each word like it pains him. "My class needs to come here. I already confirmed it with—with your boss."

"Brian," I supply helpfully.

"Yes." Another long breath. "Brian."

Silence stretches between us, heavy and strained. Once upon a time, I couldn't shut up around this man. I chatted his ear off, coming to class early every day so I could tell him all about the books I was reading. And though I can see now in hindsight that he never returned the gesture—never gave me special treatment or told me anything personal about himself—for a while there I felt so, so comfortable around him.

"Are you going to give me trouble over this, Emma?"

Mr Finch aims his question over my shoulder, his scowl deeper than I've ever seen. And that old bruise on my heart, the one I've carried around for three years… god, it *aches.* The force of it sways me on my feet.

"No," I grit out. I don't trust myself to say anything else. If I do, I'm liable to yell at this massive jerk that I'm twenty one years old, and that *he* came *here,* and the only trouble he risks around me is library late fees. The Grumpy Grandmas would have a field day over such a meltdown.

Mr Finch thinks I still love him? Ha! As if.

I wrap my arms tight around myself, hugging my middle.

"We can reserve tables for you if you send us a headcount. And if you need specific books or other materials ready in advance, you can send us those details by email."

Mr Finch looks relieved that we're back on solid ground. When that scowl eases he looks so freaking handsome.

Though honestly, he looks delicious either way. I used to live for this man's praise, but there's something electric about his disapproval too.

"Thank you, Emma." He pauses. Glances to the side, then back at me. "And listen—"

"You'll be sharing the space with our seniors' book club," I say, cutting him off. Whatever he was about to say, I'm one thousand percent sure I don't want to hear it, delicious tingles or no. Blame and recrimination? No, thank you. Awkward pity? I'd like that even less. "Your students will need to respect other library users while they're here. All the usual rules apply."

Mr Finch's mouth flattens into a line, but he nods. "Of course."

Is this weird for him? Having *me* be the one giving commands? I mean, I'm a library assistant, not an emperor, but still. *I* find this weird.

"It'll be fun." My forced brightness is too loud, too brash, and the book club shushes me. I ignore them, cheeks heating. "Your students will love it. And—and I'm sure you can handle most of the sessions on your own. I'll be around if you need anything, but you probably won't. Right?"

He nods once, curt and crisp. "Right."

God. Some time over the last few years, I forgot the exact shade of those eyes. Deep, vivid green, like a mossy bank, or the depths of a forest glade. Eyes like you've never seen before.

They bore into me, and I'm held captive. Trapped.

Mr Finch opens his mouth, then closes it again. I wait, but he doesn't speak. Shit, what was he going to say? I'm right back where I was three years ago, and I hate it: hanging on this man's every word.

"Good to see you, Emma," he settles on at last, then turns on his heel and strides away across the library lobby. A few gray heads from the book club table perk up, watching him go with blatant appreciation. If they keep staring like that, their reading glasses will fog over.

I drop into the help desk chair, my bruised heart hammering against my ribs. All around, the library is filled with the sound of turning pages and creaking chairs; soft footfalls and the *swish, thump* of books being put back on their shelves.

I need to re-shelve the books on the library cart. Need to dust and take down expired notices on the noticeboard. Need to make Brian his four-thirty coffee and check up on the grandmas and generally do my freaking job.

But my legs are wobbly. My temples throb.

Maybe I'll sit here for five minutes first.

* * *

Check out Dear Diary!

xxx

Cassie Mint

About the Author

Cassie writes outrageous, OTT instalove with tons of sugar and spice. She loves cookie dough, summer barbecues, and her gorgeous cat Missy.

You can connect with me on:

- https://www.authorcassiemint.com
- https://www.facebook.com/cassiemintauthor
- https://www.bookbub.com/authors/cassie-mint

Subscribe to my newsletter:

- https://www.authorcassiemint.com/newsletter

Printed in Great Britain
by Amazon